PEN PALS:
BOOK SEVEN

HANDLE
WITH CARE

by Sharon Dennis Wyeth

A YEARLING BOOK

Published by
Dell Publishing
a division of
Bantam Doubleday Dell Publishing Group, Inc.
666 Fifth Avenue
New York, New York 10103

ISBN: 0-440-40267-0

Published by arrangement with Parachute Press, Inc.
Printed in the United States of America
February 1990
10 9 8 7 6 5 4 3 2 1
OPM

have TO finish reading

For Lori, Shelley, Delphine, Dolores and Myisha

CHAPTER ONE

———◆———

"Hey, Shanon!" Amy Ho called from the hallway. "Come out here for a minute. Lisa found something in the common room she wants you to see."

Shanon Davis flipped her long sandy-colored braid over her shoulder and with a smile looked up at Amy. As usual, Amy's and Shanon's outfits were a study in contrast. While Shanon wore a sensible long-sleeved, high-necked cotton nightgown, Amy was using an extra-large Sting T-shirt for a nightshirt.

"I'm right in the middle of my last math problem, Amy," Shanon said. "What could Lisa possibly want now? It's almost time for lights out."

Amy and Shanon were suitemates in a dormitory called Fox Hall at the Alma Stephens School for Girls. Lisa Mc-Greevy was Shanon's roommate, while Amy shared a bedroom with a girl named Palmer Durand. All four of the girls were first-year students, or third-formers as they were called at Alma.

"I have no idea what Lisa wants," Amy said. "But she said you should hurry, so come on!"

"Oh, all right," Shanon said reluctantly. She had been feeling kind of down all day, and all she really wanted to do was climb into bed and pull the covers over her head. But she knew Lisa too well for that. If Lisa wanted Shanon to see something in the common room, Shanon would have no peace until she did exactly that.

With a sigh, Shanon closed her book and reached out for her favorite old blue bathrobe. She pulled it on over her nightgown, then followed Amy out of the suite and down the hallway.

As soon as she stepped through the door to the common room, Shanon knew something strange was going on. "Why is it so dark in here?" she began. "Where's Lisa? Why . . . ?"

"*Surprise!*"

The lights in the common room flashed on, and four girls in pajamas, nightgowns, and bathrobes jumped out from behind the couch. Shanon's hazel eyes widened in shock and surprise. The other girls took one look at her astonished expression and burst out laughing.

Just then, Lisa darted behind a tall chair and came back out with a great big gooey cake. "Happy birthday, Shanon!" she cried, her dark eyes flashing. Tall and slender, with long dark hair, Lisa was dressed for the occasion in the second-hand flowing rose-colored satin robe she'd bought at an antique clothing store. According to the salesgirl, the robe had once belonged to Madonna.

"Thirteen candles, Shanon!" Lisa said excitedly. "Count 'em!"

Shanon blinked and then grinned. "You *remembered*!" she said happily.

"Oh, come *on!*" Lisa exclaimed, carefully placing the cake in the middle of the coffee table. "You didn't really think we would forget the birthday of one of the Foxes, did you?"

The girls in Suite 3-D started calling themselves the Foxes of the Third Dimension a few weeks after school began last fall because they lived in Suite 3-D of Fox Hall. Before long, they shortened it to just the Foxes.

Palmer Durand stepped out from behind the couch and handed Shanon a small flat package. She had wavy, shoulder-length blond hair, and the powder blue of her silk nightgown and robe was a perfect match for her big beautiful eyes.

"Happy birthday, Shanon," Palmer said. "I wanted to give you something particularly special since this is such a significant birthday. You're the last one of us to turn thirteen!"

"Thanks, Palmer," Shanon said. She pulled the wrapping paper off the package and smiled. "An autographed picture of *you*! It's really nice."

"Glad you like it," Palmer said, tossing her hair away from her face. "But it's not just a picture of me—that's you bending over the water fountain. Don't you remember? Kate took it the day of the class picnic. Too bad your hair was in your—"

"Hey, come on, you guys!" Lisa called. "We're doing the presents later. Shanon hasn't even had a chance to blow out the candles, and they're melting all over the frosting!"

Shanon looked apprehensively over her shoulder. "This is really wonderful," she said in a whisper. "But aren't we all going to get into trouble? It's after hours, and we're supposed to be in bed!" She shot a worried look at a thin girl wearing glasses and a plain flannel bathrobe. It was Kate Majors, the Fox Hall dorm monitor. A fifth-former, Kate was usually a real stickler for the rules. But right now she didn't seem at all concerned as she eyed the cake hungrily.

"And what if Miss Grayson finds out about us?" Shanon went on.

"She already knows about it!" a cheerful voice said behind her. Shanon jumped and turned around to face Maggie Grayson, the young French teacher and resident faculty member of Fox Hall, who was standing in the doorway. "And she thinks it's just great!" Miss Grayson came into the room and gave Shanon a big hug. "Your roommate Lisa arranged the whole thing a few days ago," she explained. "She wanted to be sure to surprise you, and she thought you'd never suspect an 'after hours' party!"

"Well, she thought right!" Shanon laughed. "I didn't have the slightest clue this was going to happen!"

"Come *on*, Shanon!" Brenda Smith said impatiently.

"We're all dying of starvation over here!" Brenda was a fourth-former who lived in Fox Hall, too.

Smiling self-consciously, Shanon hurried over to the coffee table and bent down to blow out the candles. "Wait a minute!" Lisa yelled. "Don't forget to make a wish! But think fast—the candles are about to burn up the cake!"

"I don't have to think at all," Shanon said. "I'm going to wish that the people in this room will always be my friends. Especially you, Lisa. This is the best birthday I've ever had!"

"You haven't seen anything yet," Lisa said mysteriously.

Shanon finally blew out the candles, and everyone clapped and shouted "Happy Birthday." Then Lisa ran back around behind her chair again. This time she returned with paper plates, plastic forks, a cake knife, an ice-cream scoop, and several cartons of ice cream. "Let's see," she said. "I've got orange sherbet, strawberry-vanilla swirl, butter almond, and chocolate-chocolate chip. Place your orders now!"

Everyone grabbed a plate and crowded around the table while Lisa dished out the cake and ice cream. Soon all the girls were sitting on the floor with heaping platefuls balanced on their knees. Shanon took one bite of cake and closed her eyes. "This is undoubtedly the most delicious cake I've ever had in my entire thirteen-year-old life!" she exclaimed. "Who made it?"

Lisa flushed with pleasure. "I did," she said. "Well, that is, I made the frosting. It's German chocolate—an old recipe of my grandmother's. I tried to make the cake myself, too, but it stuck to the pans and fell all apart, and I turned the kitchen into a disaster area. Mrs. Butter helped me on the second go-round." Mrs. Butter was the girls' affectionate nickname for the school's roly-poly English cook, Mrs. Worth.

"Well, please extend my compliments to the chef!" Shanon said. "The cake and the frosting are both fantastic. I may even have another tiny slice!"

"You have to open your presents first," Amy said, pointing to a little pile of packages Shanon hadn't noticed before. Amy picked up a rectangular foil-wrapped gift. "This one's from me."

Shanon put down her cake plate and opened Amy's present. It was a handmade wooden picture frame. "This is beautiful, Amy!" Shanon said. "I'll bet you made it yourself in wood-shop class."

"That's perfect!" Palmer said. "You can use the frame for the picture I just gave you."

Amy shot Palmer a look and rolled her eyes. "I was *thinking* she could use the frame for a picture of her pen pal, Mars," she explained. "That's why I painted those pictures of pens and envelopes all around the edges like that."

Since the beginning of the school year, the girls had been writing letters to boys from the nearby Ardsley Academy. Shanon's pen pal was Arthur Martinez, or Mars, as he preferred to be called. When he and his three suitemates had first started writing, they had referred to themselves as The Unknown, and the name had stuck—even though the girls had come to know their pen pals pretty well by now.

6

Kate Majors reached over and grabbed a small, cylindrical package from the pile. "Open mine next," she said. "It kind of goes with Amy's in a way."

Shanon pulled the ribbon and paper off the package and revealed an old-fashioned black and gold fountain pen.

"It's gorgeous!" Shanon said.

"I got it for you to use for taking notes for newspaper stories," Kate explained. She and Shanon both spent a lot of time working on the school newspaper, *The Ledger*. "But I guess it's okay to use it for writing letters to your pen pal if you want."

Lisa rolled her eyes but kept her mouth shut. There was something about Kate that really annoyed her. It was just like that girl to tell Shanon what to do with her gift. But Shanon was really fond of Kate, and Lisa didn't want to spoil the party.

Brenda's present to Shanon was a pair of earplugs. "You can use them when Amy and I are practicing our music," she explained.

"But I *like* your music!" Shanon protested. "Most of the time anyway. At least when I'm not trying to study . . . or go to sleep."

Everyone laughed, and then Miss Grayson produced one long-stemmed rose and handed it to Shanon. "I remember when I turned thirteen," she said, giving Shanon a kiss on the top of her head. "It's a very special birthday."

"Oh, thank you, Miss Grayson. I love roses, but no one ever gave me one before!"

The girls went back to eating their cake for a few minutes, but then Lisa suddenly jumped to her feet again. "I can't wait any longer!" she cried. "My present to you was the party, Shanon. But I do have something else for you. It's from an absent guest." And she ran around behind her chair one more time. She came right back, holding a thick white envelope with Shanon's name on it.

At once, Shanon recognized the handwriting as her pen pal's! "How did you get a letter from Mars?" Shanon asked.

"He sent it to me to hold on to for you," Lisa explained. "He wanted to be sure you didn't open it until your birthday party."

Shanon took the envelope and looked down at it for a long moment. "Well, hurry up, Shanon!" Lisa said eagerly. "Open it up and read it!"

Shanon felt her cheeks growing warm. She knew everyone expected her to read the letter out loud, but she suddenly felt very shy. What if Mars had written something personal? He didn't do it very often, but every now and then he said something she might not want to broadcast to a roomful of people!

" I don't know," she began, clutching the envelope to her chest. "Maybe I should wait till—"

But Shanon's protest was interrupted by loud boos and hisses from the other girls. "You'd better go ahead and read it, Shanon," Amy said when the noise had died down. "We're not going to let you out of here until you do!"

"I guess you're right." Shanon smiled. And with no further argument, she opened Mars's letter and began to read.

CHAPTER TWO

———————◆———————

Dear Birthday Girl,
  Oh, lo, these many weeks have I spent trying to think of the perfect present for you, my lady of letters. Naturally, my first choice was the moon and the stars, but since my spaceship's in the shop, that was out of the question. My second choice was a romantic candlelit dinner for two at a secluded spot—

At this point in her reading, Shanon was again interrupted, this time by the gasps and squeals of her friends. She looked up from the letter, red-faced with embarrassment. "I don't know about this," she said shyly.

"You can't stop now!" Brenda cried. "It's just starting to get interesting."

"Brenda's right!" Amy chimed in. "Hurry up and read the rest before our pulse rates have a chance to slow down!"

Shanon looked at the faces surrounding her. To her surprise, she saw that even Kate Majors and Miss Grayson were leaning forward in anticipation, eagerly waiting to hear the rest of Mars's letter. She cleared her throat and started reading again.

but for some reason, the headmaster at Ardsley has nixed that idea. And so I've had to settle for my third choice—which is enclosed with this letter. Since your writing is so important to you (and to me too, for that matter!), I thought you might enjoy knowing what it really means. I hope you like it!

Happy birthday!
Mars

Shanon immediately looked inside the envelope and pulled out a folded piece of paper. She opened it up and gave a little giggle. "He's had my handwriting analyzed by an expert!" she said with delight.

"Wow!" said Amy. "Read us what it says!"

"Okay. Here it is," said Shanon.

My analysis of this handwriting specimen indicates that the writer is an extremely intelligent and creative person. She is outgoing and strong-willed, with pronounced leadership capabilities. She is daring and inventive, with a real mind of her own. The writer is also a truly passionate person, with a definite capacity for temperament. Because of her strong

11

feelings and emotional highs and lows, life with this writer would never be boring!

"Wow!" Amy breathed when Shanon had finished reading. "That's incredible. Imagine being able to figure all that stuff out, just based on somebody's handwriting!"

"I think it's a wonderful idea for a birthday present, Shanon," Miss Grayson said.

"It *is* a wonderful idea," Lisa agreed. "Though I'm not sure how accurate it is. I mean, the intelligent, creative part definitely sounds like Shanon, but the rest of it doesn't at all."

There was a moment of thoughtful silence, and then Lisa came up behind Shanon and started reading the analysis over her shoulder. "Just listen to what this says!" she continued. " 'Outgoing . . . strong-willed . . . emotional highs and lows . . . temperament . . . a leader'! These things are the opposite of you, Shanon! You're sweet and shy and easygoing. The person this guy is talking about sounds more moody, more up and down—you know, the kind of person who likes to be upfront and center stage all the time. In fact, now that I think of it, the person the analyst is describing sounds quite a bit like *me*!"

"Well, isn't that just like you, Lisa McGreevy!" Kate Majors broke in indignantly. "To hog the limelight and claim Shanon's birthday present is really all about you!"

Lisa's mouth dropped open in surprise. "Oh, for Pete's sake, Kate!" she said. "I'm not trying to hog the limelight at all—I'm just pointing out that the handwriting analysis seems a little off base to me."

"Well, I think *you're* off base!" Kate exclaimed.

"Kate," Shanon said anxiously. "Lisa. Come on." She sat in her chair and nervously twisted the edges of the handwriting analysis. Shanon hated any kind of fighting, particularly between two of her closest friends. She wished Kate and Lisa could learn to get along, but no matter how hard she tried to make peace between them, it never lasted. Shanon suspected that part of the problem involved Lisa's older brother Reggie, who attended Ardsley Academy and was always writing to Kate and looking for ways to see her. But Lisa insisted that Reggie had nothing to do with their friction.

Now Lisa and Kate were both standing in the middle of the room, glaring at each other. "Why am *I* off base," Lisa demanded indignantly, "when *you're* the one who's starting a fight right in the middle of Shanon's party?"

"I'm not starting a fight!" Kate retorted. "I'm just pointing out how, once again, you've managed to divert all the attention to yourself and your show-off personality!"

"Oh, is that right?" Lisa said. "Well, for your information—"

"*Stop!*"

Kate and Lisa both closed their mouths in surprise and turned around to face Amy, who was standing only a few inches away from them. "Will you two knock it off already? Can't you see you're ruining Shanon's birthday?"

13

Kate and Lisa both glanced over at Shanon and realized their friend was almost ready to cry. Immediately, they felt ashamed of themselves.

"I'm sorry, Shanon," Kate said. "I didn't mean to make you feel bad."

"I'm sorry, too!" Lisa cried, rushing over to Shanon's side. "Don't mind Kate and me—we were just being silly." She knelt down next to her roommate's chair. "I'm sorry if I hogged the limelight, Shanon. You should know better than to listen to me. You know I always talk without thinking. I didn't mean any of that stuff I said. In fact, I think the handwriting analysis was terrific! You really do have all the qualities the analyst says you do—leadership, passion, temperament, and tons of—"

"All *right*, Lisa!" Shanon said with a smile. "Stop apologizing. I forgive you!" She waved a hand around the room. "I forgive all of you—even though you weren't doing anything wrong!"

The other girls laughed, relieved that the fighting was over. They turned back to the remains of their cake and ice cream, chatting and giggling in between bites. Only Shanon remained silent and somber. She wasn't really angry with Lisa or Kate, she realized, but their argument had started her thinking. What exactly *had* Mars meant by sending her that handwriting analysis? She had assumed he had intended it as a compliment—but maybe he had really been making fun of her by sending her an analysis that described a person who was her exact opposite!

And what about Lisa? Shanon thought. Even though she had bent over backward with her apology, it was obvious she had *really* meant what she said in the first place. Lisa didn't think Shanon was a leader or a passionate person at all. She had *said* that Shanon was "sweet and shy and easygoing." But if you read between the lines, what did that actually mean? It actually meant that Shanon was a spineless jellyfish with a boring personality!

All at once, Shanon felt she had to know if that's what everyone thought of her. She leaned forward in her chair and interrupted a conversation between Amy and Palmer. "Amy?" she asked tentatively. "Do *you* think I'm shy?"

Amy put down her fork and stared at her. "Well," she said. "I never really thought about it before, but now that you ask, I guess the answer is yes. Not that I think there's anything wrong with being shy, of course. It isn't any big deal. It's just one of those things everybody knows about you."

"Right," Palmer said helpfully. "We all think it's nice that you're shy instead of loud and aggressive. Sort of like an adorable little kitten or something!"

Kitten! Shanon repeated miserably to herself. She felt her cheeks growing hot with shame. Palmer was probably putting it kindly. Everyone obviously thought she was a scared little mouse, afraid of her own shadow!

Miss Grayson, who had overheard the last part of the conversation, caught sight of Shanon's expression. "You have a wonderful low-keyed personality that I find very refreshing, Shanon," she said sympathetically. "After all, if everyone tried to be a prima donna, the world would be a pretty terrible place."

Without saying anything, Shanon sat back in her chair and chewed on the last bite of her cake. As she looked around the room at her friends, she realized that her good mood had vanished. Not that she wasn't grateful for her surprise party. She knew Lisa and the other girls had gone to a lot of trouble to make this birthday a success. Still, she couldn't help feeling upset by their comments. She hadn't realized till now that her very best friends considered her such a pitiful creature. Then Shanon realized something else. Not only did they all think she was spineless and timid, they hadn't even been embarrassed to tell her so, right to her face! They must *really* think she was a wimp!

CHAPTER THREE

———◆———

Late that night after everyone else was asleep, Shanon slipped out of bed and found her flashlight, her stationery, and her new pen. Then she crawled back under the quilt and started writing to Mars. She wanted to thank him for his birthday present right away. But she also felt she just couldn't wait until morning to write down some of the questions she'd been thinking about.

Dear Mars,

Thank you very much for your birthday package. My party and your present both took me completely by surprise—in more ways than one! In fact, I wasn't the only one who was surprised by the handwriting analysis you sent me. All my friends and even Miss Grayson seemed to think the analyst was describing a totally different person from me! According to them, I'm not a leader and not passionate, and I have as much temperament as a slice of white bread!

Since I'm sure you must have read the analysis before you sent it to me, I was wondering if you feel the same way they do—and if so, why you would send me something that was obviously untrue. Could you please let me know exactly what you had in mind?

Please write back soon.

Your pen pal,
Shanon

The next morning, Shanon got dressed quickly because she wanted to drop her letter in the mail slot before breakfast. She was already heading out her bedroom door when Lisa sat up in bed and stretched. "Hi, Shanon!" Lisa said sleepily. "You're certainly the early bird this morning." She rubbed her eyes and gave Shanon a closer look. "Say, why don't you wear my yellow and green sweater with that skirt instead of the plain white one you have on? That one makes you look a little washed out." She got out of bed and crossed to her bureau. "Here, I'll get it out for you."

"That's okay, Lisa," Shanon said. "I'm already dressed, and I'm in a hurry to mail this letter."

"It'll only take me a minute to find it. Let's see . . . I know it's in here somewhere. Aha! Here it is."

She carried the brightly colored sweater over to Shanon, who obediently peeled off her plain white sweater and changed clothes. Then Shanon hurried toward the door again. "Wait a minute!" Lisa called. "Do you want me to put your hair up in a French twist like I did last week? Everybody said it made you look a lot more sophisticated, remember? Now that you're thirteen, you ought to wear your hair like that all the time."

Shanon paused in the doorway, fingering the end of her long braid. "I'm kind of in a rush, Lisa," she said after a minute. "Maybe we can do it after classes. See you!" And she hurried off to mail her letter to Mars.

Two days later, right after her last class of the day, Shanon received an answer.

Dear Shanon,

I can tell from your letter that my birthday present to you was not the knockout success I'd planned. Honestly, the reason I sent you that handwriting analysis was very simple, though you may think it was simple-minded—I simply thought you'd like it! I did read the analysis before I sent it, but I just thought it was funny and interesting. I should have realized that you were a more sensitive, reserved type of person and that you might have been embarrassed and gotten your feelings hurt. I'm really truly sorry if that's what happened! Even as I write this, I'm down on my knees begging for your forgiveness! Please write back soon and let me know I haven't scared you off for life.

Your pen pal (still, I hope),
Mars

As Shanon read Mars's letter, she couldn't help smiling. Mars really was funny, she thought, and it was obvious from the way he kept apologizing that he liked her a lot. His letter was truly great.

Still smiling, Shanon sat down on a bench in the hallway outside her classroom and read the letter again. But suddenly she frowned. *Wait a minute!* she thought. Mars was talking about her in the exact same way as Lisa and everybody else at the birthday party! Look at the words he had used to describe her personality: *Sensitive! Reserved! Embarrassed!* And what about that last sentence—he was worried she might be *scared off for life!* Mars was just like all the others! He thought she was a shy, scared little mouse, too!

Shanon felt she would explode if she didn't answer Mars's letter right there on the spot. Normally, she liked to write her letters on the pale blue flowered stationery her sister Doreen had given her last Christmas, but now she didn't want to waste time going back to her room for it. She ripped a page of lined paper out of her notebook and wrote her letter on that instead.

Dear Mars,

Thank you for writing back to me so quickly. I'm sorry you think I'm so shy and timid I'd be embarrassed by something like having my handwriting analyzed! It's pretty obvious that you do agree with Lisa and the other girls—my personality is the opposite of what the analysis said. In other words, I'm not a leader (which makes me a wimpy fol-lower), I'm not strong-willed (I'm spineless), and I'm not passionate (I'm boring)! Please write back and let me know if my analysis is correct.

Shanon

After Shanon had scrawled out her letter, she felt a little better. At least she had finally expressed her anger. She realized she would have to take the time to go back to her room for an envelope anyway, but now that she had actually put her thoughts down on paper, she didn't feel in quite so much of a hurry. She waited till her classes were over, then took the letter back to Suite 3-D.

Amy was already there, sprawled on the pink loveseat, staring down at a letter in her hand. It was from her pen pal, John Adams. "Hi, Shanon!" Amy said. "I got the weirdest letter from John today. Just listen to this!"

Dear Amy,
Hi! I'm stuck on this poem, and I wonder if you can help me figure out an ending:

Youth is a hard time,
Oh, so hard, making things rhyme,
Up and down feelings come and go,
Truth—something, something, something . . .

This is where I'm stuck. Do you have any ideas? Let me know.

> *Uninspiredly yours,*
> *John*

"Wow, that's tough!" Shanon said sympathetically. "Have you thought of anything?"

"Not a thing!" Amy answered. "I'm drawing a complete and total blank. You've written some poetry, Shanon. Do you have any ideas?"

Shanon stared at John's poem over Amy's shoulder. "Well, I can see one thing," she said slowly. "He's started another acrostic—you know, having the first letter of each line spell out a word. So far he's got Y-O-U-T, so what you have to do is—"

Before she could finish her sentence, Lisa came bursting into the room. "Hi, guys!" she interrupted. "Come on, Shanon! I've just had the greatest idea for how we can rearrange our bedroom. I need you to help me push the beds up against the back wall."

"But I was just about to—"

"It'll only take a minute, Shanon! Come on!"

Shanon followed Lisa into the bedroom. An hour later, after they had finished rearranging their bedroom furniture to Lisa's satisfaction, Shanon finally found a minute to dig an envelope out of her desk. She stuffed the letter to Mars inside and went back to Booth Hall to mail it.

CHAPTER FOUR

Once again, Mars's answer came in the return mail two days later. When the Foxes had first started writing to The Unknown, they used to read their letters out loud to one another. But this time, Shanon carried the letter back to the suite and read it in the privacy of her bedroom.

Dear Shanon,

After I got your letter, I was really *sorry—sorry I ever, ever had the dumb idea of having your handwriting analyzed. I didn't "mean" anything by it! I just wanted to give you something different for your birthday! Please Believe Me!*

Anyway, I just don't understand why you're so upset. So what if you are a little shy? That's not such a bad thing to be. Probably a lot of famous people were shy when they were young—for all we know, Thomas Edison was shy.

Maybe Eleanor Roosevelt was shy! But they both went ahead and did great things in their lives! They just kept a "stiff upper lip" (as they say in England) and were brave.

Anyway, if you were a loudmouthed, pushy person, I probably wouldn't even like you—which I do! So please let's not argue about this subject anymore!

Your pen pal,
Mars

When Shanon was finished with the letter, she sighed. Mars truly was a nice person, she thought. That was undoubtedly why he was knocking himself out apologizing. But despite his good intentions, nothing had actually changed. Everybody, Mars included, still thought she was a shy mouse.

All at once, Shanon felt as if she'd go crazy if she didn't talk to somebody about her problem. Putting Mars's letter into her bureau drawer, she went out of the suite, walked down the hall, and knocked on Kate Majors's door.

"Come in!" Kate called. As usual, Shanon found her friend bent over a pile of books on her desk. But when Kate looked up and saw Shanon's gloomy face, she closed her notebook with a snap.

"What's the matter, Shanon?" Kate asked. "Are you sick or something?"

"Well, in a way I am," Shanon answered. "I'm sick of everybody thinking I'm a shy little wimp!"

Kate raised her eyebrows and stuck a strand of her fine

brown hair behind her ear. "Well, *I* certainly don't think you're a wimp!" she said emphatically. She gestured for Shanon to sit down. Then her eyes narrowed suspiciously behind her glasses. "Just whom have you been talking to?"

"Oh, nobody in particular," Shanon said. "I've just figured it out, that's all. Everybody thinks I'm scared of my own shadow. And the worst thing is, I'm starting to believe they're right! What do *you* think, Kate?"

Kate chewed on the end of her pencil. "You know what I think," she said after a minute. "I think that in reality you aren't all that shy. You just *seem* to be shy . . . in comparison."

Shanon frowned and sat forward in her chair. "What do you mean 'in comparison'?" she asked.

"I mean that people who show off all the time tend to get more attention than the people around them. And you live with a first-class show-off!"

For a few seconds, Shanon looked puzzled. Then she caught her breath and felt her face flush. "I know you're talking about Lisa, Kate!" she said. "And I don't think you're being fair. Lisa may be lively . . . and vivacious and colorful . . . and outgoing—but she's *not* a show-off!"

"Well, you're entitled to your opinion," Kate said dryly. "And please remember you did ask me for mine."

"Well, I'm sorry I did!" Shanon said. "You know Lisa's my friend—my best friend!" And getting quickly to her feet, she said an abrupt good night to Kate and headed out the door.

25

Shanon's first instinct was to go back to the suite and tell Lisa exactly what Kate had just said about her. But then she decided that wasn't such a good idea. Lisa and Kate already had enough problems with each other. There was no point in encouraging a real feud between them. If Lisa knew Kate had been bad-mouthing her, she'd undoubtedly stomp down the hall and create a big noisy scene right in front of everybody. . . .

As Shanon realized what she'd just been thinking, she came to a dead stop. Lisa *did* like to create scenes sometimes! And, come to think of it, there was no denying that she also *did* like to show off! And besides that, she'd been incredibly bossy lately. Just this week, Lisa had practically ordered Shanon to change her clothes and her hairstyle and even the furniture in their bedroom! And she was always interrupting Shanon's conversations with other people, as if what Lisa had to say was *guaranteed* to be more important and interesting than anything anyone else could possibly offer!

All at once, Shanon was angry—but not at Kate! Kate was right, she told herself. No wonder everybody thought Shanon was a wimpy, scared little follower with no backbone. It was because *Lisa* always had to be the bossy leader!

CHAPTER FIVE

———◆———

When Shanon returned to the suite, she found Amy struggling over a new song she was trying to finish, and Palmer writing a questionnaire to send to her pen pal, Sam O'Leary.

At the beginning of the year, when the girls had first started writing to their pen pals, they had all sent questionnaires to the boys in an effort to learn about their likes, dislikes, and interests. Since then, however, Palmer had given up her original Ardsley pen pal and started writing to Sam, a former Ardie, who had transferred to the public school in town, and was the leader of a rock group called The Fantasy. After one brief meeting, Palmer already thought Sam was the most handsome, talented musician she'd ever met, but the truth was, she barely knew him.

"What kind of questions do you think I should ask?" Palmer said, looking up from the desk.

"Why don't you just use the same questionnaire we sent to The Unknown?" Amy suggested.

"I thought I'd use some of those questions," Palmer replied, "but I want to throw in a few more interesting ones, too. The only problem is, I can't think of any," she admitted. "Do you think he'd mind if I asked him about other girls he's dated?" Palmer said.

"Well, I'm not sure you—" Shanon began.

"Don't do it!" Lisa said, coming out of the bedroom in time to hear Palmer's question. "I just read an article in a magazine that said men *hate* being asked about their pasts!" She saw Shanon and reached into the back pocket of her jeans. "Here, Shanon," she said. "I had some extra change at the vending machine so I bought you a Good 'n Plenty."

Shanon reached out to take the candy, but suddenly she pulled her fingers away from Lisa's. "I don't care for a snack right now, thank you," she said coolly.

Lisa blinked in surprise. "Okay," she said, tossing the candy on the desk. "I was sure you'd want it because it's your favorite kind and they don't usually have it in the machine, but if you're saving your appetite for dinner, it's okay with me." She glanced down at the watch on her wrist. "Hey!" she said. "It *is* almost time for dinner. We'd better go change. Come on, Shanon. You can borrow the new purple hair clips my mom just sent me."

For a second, Shanon almost followed Lisa into the bedroom. Then she stopped and folded her arms across her chest. "No, thank you," she said again. "The truth is, I'm

not planning to do anything different with my hair tonight."
Now it was her turn to glance at her watch. "And since it
is getting so near dinnertime, I think I'd better go now. I'm
walking over with Kate, and she hates being late!"

Shanon marched out of the room, and Lisa, Amy, and
Palmer stared after her. "What's bugging her?" Lisa asked
the other two girls.

"I'm not sure," Amy answered, absentmindedly fiddling
with the end of her long black and red feathered earring.
"She has been kind of touchy ever since her birthday party."

"Well, if she'd rather eat dinner with Kate Majors than
with us, she's way beyond touchy," Lisa declared. "She's
totally out of her mind!"

The next morning, when Lisa woke up, the first thing she
noticed was that Shanon's bed was already neatly made.
When she glanced out the window to check the weather, she
saw her roommate walking over toward the main building.
Kate Majors was right by her side.

Over the next several days, Shanon started spending more
and more time with Kate. The two girls went to the library
together, ate meals together, and did their homework together in Kate's room. Lisa became lonely, and she started
to feel a little bit jealous of Kate. She and Shanon had been
best friends almost since their first day at Alma, and she had
no idea what she had done to offend her.

Inside, Lisa felt very hurt. But on the surface, she kept up
her usual happy-go-lucky attitude. On Wednesday night
after dinner when all her roommates were in the suite, she

announced that she was going on an after-hours raid to the kitchen.

"I heard a rumor that Mrs. Butter baked scones this afternoon," she said. "I want to get some while they're still fresh. Who wants to come?"

"Not me," Amy said. "I pigged out on the beef stew tonight, and my stomach feels like a bowling ball!"

"Count me out, too," Palmer said. "I already had two chocolate bars from the vending machine."

Lisa looked at Shanon, who was studiously bent over her Latin book. But Shanon didn't even glance up.

"Okay, all you chickens!" Lisa said, looking away from her roommate. " 'Then I'll do it myself!' said the little red hen!"

At ten o'clock that night, when the other girls were already in bed, Lisa put on her black sweatpants and sweater and slipped out of the suite. Fifteen minutes later she returned with a bulging brown paper bag and found Shanon sitting on the couch, waiting for her.

"Still up, Shanon?" Lisa asked in surprise. "Did you decide you were hungry after all? Well, that's great because I got enough for all of us. I even managed to swipe some of the jam and clotted cream in a paper cup and—"

"I'm not hungry, Lisa," Shanon said shortly.

"Really? Okay, then you can watch me eat, and we can—"

"I don't want to watch you eat either! I want to go to bed, but I felt I had to stay up to warn you. I'm not going to tell anybody what you've done tonight—how many rules you've broken, what kind of trouble you could have gotten into, or exactly what you've *stolen* from the kitchen. But I don't want you doing it again. If you do, I'm going to tell Miss Grayson!"

With that, Shanon stood up and headed for the bedroom. Lisa stared after her, in amazement. Then, without even opening her paper bag full of scones, she went into Amy and Palmer's room and shook Amy awake.

"Wha . . . what?" Amy asked sleepily. "Is it morning already? Are we having a fire drill?"

"No! But I have to talk to someone or *I'll* be on fire! You won't believe what Shanon just did!"

"Don't tell me she went on the food raid with you!"

"Are you kidding? She did the exact opposite! When I got back, she was waiting up for me like some kind of army officer on guard duty. She actually gave me a warning never to sneak over to the kitchen again! She said she'd tell Miss Grayson if I did!"

Amy's almond-shaped eyes opened wide. "Wow!" she said. "I'm sure she only did it because she was worried about you. That doesn't sound at all like Shanon!"

"No kidding! But I know who it *does* sound like! It sounds just like our resident drill sergeant, Kate Majors! Shanon's been spending so much time with that girl she's starting to act just like her!"

"Oh, I wouldn't say that," Amy protested sleepily. "Shanon's your *friend,* Lisa! I'm sure she'll have forgotten all about it by morning." She yawned and let her head fall back

31

on the pillow. Almost immediately, she was sound asleep again.

But Lisa couldn't even think about going to sleep. She was much too upset. She crept into the sitting room, snapped on a small desk light, and sat down to write a letter to her pen pal, Rob Williams.

Dear Rob,

If I get caught writing to you now, I'll be in big trouble since it's after hours. And these days I have to be extra careful because Shanon now sees herself as some kind of professional Rule Enforcer. Tonight she actually warned me that she might turn me in *if I broke another rule! Can you believe it?*

It's all Kate Majors's fault. She and Shanon have been hanging out together since Shanon's birthday, and the two of them are like sisters now. You know how Kate and my brother Reggie write to each other? Well, the other day I asked Shanon to find out what was in their letters, and she just about bit my head off! You would have thought I'd asked her to commit treason against the government—when in fact, Kate is really the enemy!

Sorry if I sound like I'm in a bad mood. That's because I am! Roommates are truly the pits! But I miss mine—the old Shanon, that is. I wish I knew what was going on with her.

Lonesomely yours,
Lisa

A few days later, Lisa found an answer from Rob in her mailbox.

Dear Lisa,

Thanks for your letter. Even when you're complaining, it's still fun to hear from you. I do have one thing to say that you may not want to hear, though. I know you don't like Kate Majors much, but if she and Reggie want to write each other, that's really between the two of them, isn't it? I think you should definitely MYOB (mind your own business!) about that.

But I do agree with you about the other stuff you wrote. Roommates can be beyond *the pits! You wouldn't believe what my roommate's been up to lately. Mars has himself this noisy green and yellow Amazon parrot. The dumb bird actually can talk, but mostly it just screeches and squawks and throws seeds all over our room. Gross as that is, I could put up with it. But, as usual, Mars has to take things one step further. He's teaching the bird (whose name is Ricardo) all kinds of weird tricks, like turning on the lights and picking peanuts out of his pocket. But the latest gimmick is really absurd. He's got Ricardo repeating questions and answers to Trivial Pursuit questions!*

To make matters worse, we've got hordes of other guys trooping in here all day to check out "Mars's birdbrain"! I'm trying to concentrate on my homework, which has been giving me some major problems lately. But our room is like some kind of three-ring circus—with Mars as the ringleader!

To add insult to injury, while Mars is spending all his time putting on this goofy show for everybody's amusement, he's still managing to ace everything in every single class! The guy's driving me bananas!

In conclusion, I'll say it again. Roommates can be the pits! If I didn't have you to write to, I'd really be down. Please answer soon. I need all the friends I can get!

Your persecuted pen pal,
Rob

When Lisa finished reading Rob's letter, she laughed out loud. "Listen to this, Shanon!" she called to her roommate, who'd just come through the door. "Wait till you hear what your friend Mars has been up to. That guy is *such* a show-off!"

She read Shanon most of the letter, carefully leaving out all references to her or Kate. "Isn't that a scream?" she asked. "Mars is always doing something weird. But this Ricardo business is strictly for the birds!"

But Shanon wasn't laughing. For a moment there was an uncomfortable silence. Then Shanon took a deep breath and said, "I think Rob is being really mean! Ricardo sounds adorable to me," as she pulled a letter from her own pen pal out of her pocket. "Just listen to this!"

Dear Shanon,
The most incredible thing happened last night. Remember I told you about my new pet parrot, Ricardo? Well, he's

turning out to be a lot smarter than I thought possible! Last night a bunch of the guys were playing Trivial Pursuit in our suite and somebody got the question, "How many stomachs does a cow have?" Well, before anyone had time to say a word, Ricardo squawks out, "Four!" which is absolutely correct! I mean, I knew he could say the question and answer all together, but I didn't know he could actually respond to the question like that. I think we may be talking bird history here!

Shanon stopped reading and looked up at Lisa. "So you see," she said, "the bird really *is* special. Mars has always been interested in animals, and he's curious about their behavior. He can't help it if he's intelligent and inventive—and funny! What's happened to Rob's sense of humor, anyway?"

Shanon put the letter back into her pocket and started for the door. As she opened it, she turned around to face her roommate again. "And another thing, Lisa," she said quietly. "Mars is *not* a show-off. Maybe you should think about *yourself* a little bit before you accuse somebody else of that!"

CHAPTER SIX

———◆———

A few days later, Shanon and Kate were walking down the corridor in Booth Hall. Kate stopped and pointed toward a big, brightly colored poster on the bulletin board.

"*Alma Needs* YOU!" Kate read. "*Run For Third-Form Dorm Rep! Student Council Elections Next Week! Only Leaders With Good Ideas Need Apply!*" Kate stopped reading and looked at Shanon. "Leaders with good ideas," she said. "That sounds like you, Shanon."

"Yeah, right, Kate," Shanon said timidly. "I know I've been going around saying I'd *like* to be a leader, but that doesn't mean I really am one. And besides, I'm sure a lot of girls will want to be dorm rep. There's bound to be a big campaign and everything. I'd probably have to stand up and make a speech! I'd just die if I had to do that!" she added.

Kate laughed. "I don't think so," she said. "I think you'd do just fine, and you know why? Because you'd actually have something to say to the other girls. You're full of great ideas about this school, Shanon! You're always telling me things you'd like to see changed—you know, like allowing qualified third-formers to take classes with upperclassmen, or letting the students decide what colors to paint the halls, or letting them do school service to earn extra town trips—I could go on and on!"

Shanon chewed on the end of her braid and looked thoughtful. "Well, it *is* true I'd like to see some changes around here," she said slowly. "And I *have* been waiting for a chance to prove I can be a leader. . . . All right! I'll do it! Quick, show me where to sign up before I lose my nerve!"

"You don't have to sign up anywhere," Kate explained, giving her friend a brief hug. "All you have to do is be nominated at the next dorm meeting. And I can take care of that."

"How?" asked Shanon, immediately looking worried again. "Don't you have to be a third-former to make the nomination?"

"No problem," Kate replied confidently. "I'll get one of the younger girls to do it—and I'll tell her exactly what to say!"

"Thanks, Kate," Shanon said with a quick smile. "And if I try to back out of this before then, please don't let me! I really want to do this!" The two girls headed toward the dining room, still talking about the elections. They were barely out of sight when Lisa and Palmer came around the corner and stopped in front of the same bulletin board.

"Look at that," Palmer said, pointing at the poster. "They're having dorm rep elections soon."

"I know," Lisa said happily. "I want to start my campaign right away!"

"I thought you had to be nominated first," Palmer said. "Do you want me to do it?"

"Thanks," Lisa said. "But I've already talked Amy into doing it at the dorm meeting tomorrow night." She laughed. "I practically wrote the nominating speech for her. She's going to say that I'm a good speaker, a natural leader, and that I already know practically everybody who lives in Fox Hall. I also told her to mention that I was class president at my old school, so it's clear that I actually have political experience!" She brushed her dark hair away from her face. "The way I see it, if Amy gives me a good nominating speech, I'll have the election sewn up before the campaign even starts! The only other person I've heard about who's running is Muffin Talbot, and she's so quiet, hardly anybody even knows who she is! Running against her will be a cinch!"

Palmer looked at the clock on the wall. "Well, you won't be able to walk, much less run, if you starve to death!" she said. "We're already late for lunch!" And giggling, the two girls ran off down the hall.

The next evening at eight o'clock, Lisa sat expectantly on the couch in the Fox Hall common room, waiting for the dorm meeting to start. Out of habit, she looked around for

Shanon. When she saw her friend across the room laughing with Kate Majors, she quickly turned away and started talking to Palmer.

A few minutes later, Kate stood up and called the meeting to order. She asked for old business, and there was a brief discussion about the amount of noise in the halls during evening study hours. Then Kate cleared her throat.

"The next item on the agenda," she said, "is to nominate the candidates for third-form dorm rep. As you all know, this is an important position. Fox Hall's third-form rep has the responsibility for taking your concerns and ideas to Student Council—she will be your voice in the student government of this school. So think carefully before you make your nominations. The girl you pick should be a leader who's not afraid to speak out about your ideas. But she should also have some good ideas of her own."

Kate sat down and picked up a clipboard and a pen. "We will now accept nominations from the floor," she said.

Almost immediately, Muffin Talbot's roommate, Cindy Garth, jumped up and nominated Muffin.

"Thank you, Cindy," Kate said, writing Muffin's name down. "Muffin Talbot's name has now been placed into nomination. Are there any other nominations?"

Amy's hand shot up immediately.

"Yes, Amy?" Kate asked.

"I'd like to nominate Lisa McGreevy!"

Palmer and a few other girls clapped, but Shanon gasped and flushed. She'd had no idea her roommate was planning

39

to run for dorm rep! Of course she and Lisa hadn't been having too many heart-to-heart talks lately. In fact, she hadn't mentioned her own political plans to anyone but Kate.

"Lisa is a terrific leader," Amy went on, "and we all know she isn't afraid to speak her mind!"

Everyone laughed, and then Amy added, "She knows practically everybody in the whole school, plus she was class president at the school she went to last year. So that's why I'm placing her name in nomination—not to mention the fact that she said she'd short-sheet my bed if I didn't!"

There was another burst of laughter, and then the room grew quiet. A girl named Caroline Kroll, who occasionally helped out at *The Ledger,* stood up. Kate looked over at Shanon and winked as Caroline announced, "I'm placing Shanon Davis's name into nomination."

A moment of silence followed Caroline's announcement. Some of the girls in the room weren't exactly sure who Shanon was. Those who did know her were surprised that such a quiet girl would be running for office—and against her best friend!

But Caroline wasn't finished yet. "Most of you have read Shanon's columns in the school paper this year," she added. "So you know how many good ideas she has about the way Alma Stephens ought to be run. What you might not know is that, although Shanon is a quiet, easy-going person on the outside, on the inside, she's always thinking. She's got great leadership potential, and that's why I'm nominating her!"

40

A few girls clapped politely and then Caroline sat down again. When there were no further nominations, Kate started explaining the schedule for the campaign and the elections. But neither Shanon nor Lisa heard a word she said. They just sat there in shock, frozen in their chairs, staring across the room at each other.

How could this be happening? they were both asking themselves. How could they be running against each other and not even know about it? What on earth had happened to the close friendship they had shared such a short time ago?

CHAPTER SEVEN

As she brushed her teeth in the bathroom that night, Shanon stared at her reflection in the mirror. What are you doing? she asked herself. Running against somebody quiet like Muffin Talbot was one thing. But how could she possibly compete against someone as popular as Lisa? Lisa would undoubtedly win the election with one hand tied behind her back. And, to be honest, even Shanon believed that outspoken Lisa would probably be a better dorm rep than someone like herself. Besides, Lisa was her friend! Maybe she should just drop out of the race right now and become Lisa's campaign manager instead.

Shanon quickly undid her braid, brushed out her hair, and turned around to leave the bathroom. As she walked out the door, she almost crashed into Lisa, who was just coming in.

"Hi, Shanon," Lisa said.

"Hi," Shanon answered shyly.

For a few seconds, the two girls stood outside the bathroom door, looking at each other. Then Lisa smiled.

"I guess we took each other by surprise at the meeting tonight, didn't we?"

"I guess we did," Shanon said. "I'm sorry I didn't tell you I was running for dorm rep. I don't know why I didn't—I guess the subject just never came up, or something. But I want you to know I wouldn't have done it if I'd had any idea you were going to be running, too! In fact, I've just decided—"

"Well, of course I feel the same way," Lisa broke in. "Come back in the bathroom with me and maybe we can figure out what to do."

With a sudden feeling of relief, Shanon followed her roommate back into the bathroom and stood by the sink while Lisa carefully examined an almost invisible splotch on her cheek. "I'm really sorry about all of this," Lisa said after a minute. "And I'd be even sorrier if you got your feelings hurt in the election. I mean I'm sure you have loads of good ideas for things you'd want to do as dorm rep, but you know how kids are. They're not going to pay a whole lot of attention to the actual issues and . . ." Her voice trailed off as she caught sight of Shanon's face reflected in the mirror.

"What exactly are you trying to say, Lisa?" Shanon asked.

"Oh, nothing really. Just that I thought you might have changed your mind about being in the election now that you know who you'll be running against. I mean, I'm sure

Muffin Talbot is having second thoughts. You know how she is. She's kind of—"

"Kind of quiet? Kind of shy? Kind of like *me?*"

Lisa turned away from the mirror and stared at her friend. Shanon's face was flushed with embarrassment or anger— Lisa wasn't sure which. But her soft hazel eyes were definitely filled with tears.

All at once, Lisa felt just awful. "I didn't mean that at all," she began. "I just don't want you to get hurt."

"What you meant was that you think you're such a sure bet to win by a landslide, that Muffin and I might as well not even bother to run, isn't that it?"

Lisa started putting toothpaste on her toothbrush. "Well, you do have to admit I know a lot more people in the dorm than you do, Shanon."

"B-but that's not what this election is about!" Shanon stammered. "It's about who'd make the better dorm rep! It's about electing somebody with good ideas who'd be a good leader! And I just want you to know that you're not the only person in the world who fits that d-description!"

CHAPTER EIGHT

———◆———

Dear Mars,

Lately I feel like I'm becoming one of those people with two personalities! Part of me is happy and excited about being in the election and trying to organize my ideas about what I'd do as dorm rep. But the other part of me is a nervous wreck, terrified by the idea of making speeches, scared to meet people—and positive my overconfident, popular roommate is going to beat me, hands down.

Anyway, I'm trying to think of ways to campaign so people will get to know about me and my ideas, but so far all I've come up with are posters, which are kind of boring. Can you think of anything better?

Your politically perturbed pen pal,
Shanon

Dear Shanon,

Have no fear! Mars is here! I've just elected myself your long-distance campaign manager. You supply the good ideas for your dorm, and I'll supply the hype—though honestly I don't think you need much of that, and I don't think you should be nervous. After all, you were scared to even enter the race, but you went ahead and took that plunge, didn't you? Now all you have to do is concentrate on getting your ideas across.

I do know one thing you could try, though. Last semester a guy here who was running for office put a suggestion box outside his door. He asked the other kids to write down their complaints, ideas, and suggestions—signed or unsigned, whatever they preferred—and said he'd incorporate the best ones into his campaign platform. Not bad, huh? I'll let you know if I think of anything else.

Your campaign comrade,
Mars

Dear Rob,

I'm not really nervous about this dorm election thing, but lately I've been wondering if there isn't something else I should be doing about it. Shanon spends all her time hunched over a bunch of papers, and whenever anybody asks her what she's doing, she says she's "working" on her campaign. Do you have any idea what she might be doing?

46

Sorry it took me so long to answer your last letter, but this election business really has me going.

Lisa

Dear Lisa,
   The coach says if I don't get a better grade in math this time around, he might keep me off the team. What a bummer! I'll write a longer letter soon.

Rob

P.S. *Sorry, I don't know the first thing about campaigns!*

Dear John,
   I'm sorry I haven't been able to come up with any more lines for your poem. I'm sending you a tape of the song I've been trying to write. As you can see, I'm stuck, too. Any ideas for what I could do next?

Yours truly,
Amy

P.S. *Nice weather we've been having lately, right?*

Dear Amy,
   I hope this doesn't bore you, but I don't have anything else to write about except my poem. Sorry—I guess we both have writer's block!

Best wishes,
John

P.S. *Yes, the weather's been just fine.*

Amy put John's letter back inside its envelope and sighed. Then she picked up her guitar and struck a jangling chord. "I think John's bored with being my pen pal," she announced glumly. "He says, 'I hope this doesn't bore you,' right here in this letter."

"That's not the same thing as saying he's bored himself," Palmer commented distractedly from her chair in the corner. She had just received a thick letter from Sam O'Leary, and her nose was buried in it. Sam had finally filled out the answers to the questionnaire she'd sent him, and she was eagerly devouring his answers.

"What do *you* think, Shanon?" Amy asked. "Do you think John is bored with writing to me?"

"Uh . . . hmmmm?" Shanon put down her birthday pen and stared at Amy. "Uh . . . what's that you asked, Amy?"

Amy opened her fingers and John's letter fluttered to the floor. "Oh, never mind," she said. "It's not important. What are you working on so hard over there?"

"Well, I've just been going over these suggestions from the suggestion box I put out in the hall."

"That was really a terrific idea, Shanon," Amy said enthusiastically. "Have you gotten a lot of responses?"

Shanon pointed to a big pile of papers in front of her. "I've gotten a ton," she said. "Of course, some of them are totally off the wall—for example, one girl says third-formers should be served breakfast in bed each morning because they're under so much pressure!" She pawed through the papers. "But some of the suggestions are really intelligent.

Here's one from a girl who wants to start a flower garden outside the dorm. She suggests raising money for the bulbs and seeds with a cake sale and then having the girls do all the work taking care of the garden."

"That sounds like fun!" Amy said. "We could spell out our names with daffodils or something wild like that!"

Just then, Lisa came through the door, and somehow, the atmosphere in the room immediately changed. Amy felt herself tensing up. The suite had been like a war zone lately, she thought to herself. Shanon and Lisa, the two roommates who'd been the closest in the past, were hardly speaking to each other now. And when they did have something to say, it wasn't always pleasant.

Sometimes Amy felt she was being torn in half by the two of them. On the one hand, since she was the one who'd nominated Lisa for Student Council in the first place, Amy felt she owed Lisa some loyalty. On the other hand, Shanon really did have a lot of good ideas about what a dorm rep could do, and she was obviously giving the campaign a lot of serious thought and hard work!

Amy sighed again. None of the campaign stuff would matter, she suddenly realized, if only Shanon and Lisa could act like friends again!

"What sounds like fun?" Lisa asked, plopping her books down on the desk.

"Oh, just one of the suggestions Shanon got from her suggestion box," Amy explained. "Somebody thinks we ought to start a freshman flower garden."

"Ugh!" Lisa scoffed. "As if third-formers don't have enough pressures and problems without having to worry about gross stuff like root rot, snails, and slugs!"

There was a moment of charged silence. Then Shanon got to her feet. "I think it's a wonderful idea," she said. "It's just the kind of project that would take kids' minds *off* all their pressures and problems."

"You've got to be kidding!" Lisa responded. "With all the homework, tests, and studying we have, you think girls are going to want to waste time grubbing around outside in the mud?"

"Yes, I do," Shanon insisted. "I think—"

"*I* think the two of you should be quiet for a minute!" Palmer said huffily. "You know this election isn't the *only* thing going on in the world. Other people have problems, too! But a person can't hear herself think around here lately with the two of you debating everything all the time!"

Lisa and Shanon stared at each other sheepishly. Then they both turned toward Palmer. "We're sorry, Palmer," they said in one voice.

"Well, you ought to be!" Palmer pouted. "Here I am with this really incredible questionnaire from Sam to deal with, and not one of you is even the teeniest bit interested in it! Last fall when the original pen pals filled out questionnaires, we all sat around and talked about every single answer. But nobody's even asked me what Sam wrote!"

"Sorry, Palmer," Shanon said again. "I guess we have been a little caught up in the election."

"Caught up?" Palmer repeated, raising her eyebrow. "You're not caught up—you're obsessed! None of you cares about anything else, not even your pen pals! In fact, Amy hardly even *has* a pen pal anymore. She and John are writing to each other about the weather, for Pete's sake! And, Lisa and Shanon, all you two do is fight about your silly campaigns. Here I am with a really serious problem, and no one will even talk to me about it. I don't know Sam very well yet, but I know I want him to like me—and I don't have the slightest idea what kind of letters to write to him!"

Amy glanced at Lisa and Shanon, who glanced at each other and then quickly looked down at the floor. "What I want to know," Palmer continued, "is whatever happened to our whole pen pals plan? Am I the only one who still wants one?"

"Okay, okay, okay," Lisa said. "Let's all forget about the election for a while. Is that all right with you, Shanon?"

"It's more than all right," Shanon said, sweeping her papers aside. "I'm tired of talking politics all the time. Let's talk about *boys* for a change!"

"I'll second that motion," Lisa said, flashing Shanon a grin.

"Great," Shanon said. "Why don't you read us Sam's latest letter right now, Palmer."

"That's more like it!" Palmer said. "Here goes."

Dear Palmer,
Here's my completed questionnaire—I don't know what

the answers mean, but I hope you like it anyway! I hardly had time to fill it out, what with my weekend job and rehearsing with the band and all. Somehow my life's gotten a lot busier since I left Ardsley and transferred back to public school here in town. You wouldn't believe how different things are out in the real world!

Let me know what you think of my questionnaire answers. Some of the questions were a little personal—which is okay with me if you promise not to tell your roommates what I said!

> *I wish I could see you again,*
> *Sam*

For a few minutes, the election was totally forgotten as all the girls reacted to Sam's letter. "Wow!" Amy said. "Just how personal were your questions, Palmer?"

Palmer blushed. "Sorry, girls." She giggled. "You heard what he said—I'm not supposed to tell my roommates!"

"*Palm*-er!" Amy shrieked. "You'd better tell. We're not just your roommates—we're the Foxes!"

"That's right, Palmer," Lisa said. "We girls have to stick together!"

"Please, Palmer," Shanon coaxed. "Just tell us a few of his answers! You know we won't stop bothering you till you do."

"Well, if you insist," Palmer said slyly. She shuffled through the papers in her hand. "I'll give you three of Sam's answers, but no more. Okay?"

"Okay!" the other girls cried.

"Let's see . . . I asked him what his favorite color was . . . and he said it was bright red."

"Far out!" Amy screamed. "He must be really passionate!"

Palmer's face turned Sam's favorite color. "I certainly hope so!" she said, skipping over another question. "Hmmm . . . I asked him what kind of car he'd be if he were a car, and he said a Jeep Renegade."

"Oh, I just love Jeeps." Shanon sighed. "They're great-looking and so rugged."

"Sort of like Clint Eastwood." Lisa giggled. "Come on, Palmer," she cried as Palmer began slowly folding up the questionnaire. "Read us one more. You promised!"

"Okay, okay. I asked him what part of a girl's face he noticed first when he looked at her."

"And what did he say?" Amy demanded.

Palmer rolled her big blue eyes. "He said he noticed her eyes—especially if they were the same color as the sky!"

The other girls stared at one another and laughed hysterically. "You'd better watch out for this guy, Palmer!" Amy said when she could finally talk. "He sounds *sooo* cool!"

"Well, I think Sam sounds really romantic," Shanon said. "And a lot more grown-up than most boys. After all, he has a job and plays in a band, too! He *is* part of the real world!"

"I like the way he closed the letter—'I wish I could see you again,' " Lisa said.

"I wish I could see *him* again!" Palmer said wistfully. "But how can I? Alma Stephens sometimes has joint events with Ardsley Academy, but never with the Brighton public school!"

"Maybe you could get permission to meet him sometime," Amy said.

"Wouldn't that be wonderful?" Palmer said. "But he'd have to ask me first."

"I bet he will," Shanon said encouragingly.

"Maybe," Palmer said. "I'd just like to know for sure. I wish I could see into the future!"

CHAPTER NINE

———◆———

The girls continued to talk about Sam and Palmer, and before long they were laughing and joking just as they had in the old days, before the election campaigns began to complicate everything. They were still in a good mood at dinnertime, and they decided to order a giant Monstro pizza from Figaro's.

When the pizza arrived, they put the flat, greasy box in the center of the floor and sat down in a circle to eat. Shanon reached for the first piece and bit into it. "Let's play a game or something," she said as she chewed. "I have Trivial Pursuit in the closet."

Lisa shot Shanon a look, remembering Mars's and Rob's letters on that subject. But before she could say anything, Amy hastily spoke up. "What about that game we played with Brenda a few months ago?" she suggested. "You know, that one called Botticelli, where you give the first initial of a famous person's last name and everybody asks questions in categories to try to figure out who it is?"

"Good idea!" Palmer said. "I have somebody in mind already. The first initial of her last name is *B*."

"Thanks, Palmer," Lisa said. "You already let us know it's a female."

Shanon grinned and said, "Now let's see . . . is your famous person a composer?"

"No," Palmer said.

"That's not how you play, Palmer!" Amy explained. "You're supposed to think of a composer whose name starts with *B* and say, 'No, it's not Beethoven.' But if you can't think of a composer, then Shanon gets to ask you a direct question about the person you're thinking of!"

"Wow, that's complicated," Palmer said. "Anyway, okay, it's not Beethoven!"

Everyone laughed, and then Lisa took a turn. "Is your famous person a tennis player?"

"Ah . . . ummm . . . no, it's not Bjorn Borg!"

"Wait a minute!" Shanon said. "I bet I know who it is! I bet it's Christie Brinkley, the model!"

Palmer's mouth dropped open. "You're right, Shanon!" she said. "How in the world did you guess that?"

"Well, I noticed her picture on the front of that *Vogue* magazine you were reading this afternoon. And besides, people are always telling you that you look like her, so I figured that was probably it."

"Far out, Shanon!" Amy exclaimed. "You're really good at this! I mean, I knew you were smart, but I didn't know you had ESP!"

As Amy gave Shanon a quick hug, Lisa said, "I have somebody in mind. The first initial of his last name is W."

"Let's see," Amy began. "Is it a former President of the United States?"

"No, it's not . . . Woodrow Wilson!"

"Is it a famous American pop artist?" Shanon asked.

"No, it's not . . ." Lisa shrugged. "I can't think of anyone."

"Andy Warhol!" Shanon said. "Now I get to ask a real question. Is your person living?"

"Yes, he is!" Lisa laughed. "He's the living end!"

"Wait a minute," Amy said suspiciously. "Your pen pal's last name starts with W. Are you thinking of Rob Williams?"

Lisa giggled and nodded.

"But you were supposed to pick somebody famous!" Palmer protested.

"Well, you've all heard of him, haven't you?" Lisa said.

"I guess so," Palmer agreed good-naturedly. "So that means my famous person is a really great-looking musician who wishes he could see me!"

"And mine is a frustrated poet who writes boring letters!" Amy giggled.

"And mine is a guy with a name from outer space!" Shanon chimed in.

They all laughed and reached into the pizza box for seconds.

"I think we all know who we're thinking about," Amy said as she peeled a piece of pepperoni off her slice and popped it into her mouth.

"Well, I have somebody you might not guess so easily," Lisa said. "Not one of our pen pals. It's a woman of letters whose last name starts with *D*."

The other three girls chewed thoughtfully and stared at each other. "Gosh," Amy said after a minute. "I can't think of a single woman writer whose name starts with *D*."

"I'll give you a hint," Lisa said helpfully. "She's sort of a junior Kate Majors."

All at once, Shanon threw the remains of her pizza back in the box and jumped to her feet. "I can't believe it, Lisa!" she cried. "I can't believe you'd use this game as a chance to insult me again!"

Everyone stared at Lisa, and her face slowly turned bright red. "I wasn't trying to insult you, Shanon," she said feebly. "It was just a joke. You and Kate have been hanging out together an awful lot lately, and—"

"And I know exactly how you feel about Kate!" Shanon burst out. "You can't stand her. So I guess this means you can't stand me either!"

Lisa swallowed hard and tried to think of something to say, but for the moment she was at a complete loss for words.

Shanon deliberately turned her back on Lisa and said to

Amy, "Please tell my *former* friend Lisa McGreevy that I am *not* a junior Kate Majors! I'm not a junior anybody. I am myself, and that's perfectly all right with me!" And with that, she spun around, ran out of the sitting room and into the bedroom, slamming the door behind her.

The other three girls stared after her in shocked silence. "Whew!" Lisa finally said. "I don't think I've ever seen Shanon so angry. Have you noticed how temperamental she's getting to be lately!"

Amy got to her feet and looked down at Lisa. "Well, if she is," she said unhappily, "I think it's mostly your fault, Lisa. Why did you have to be so mean, just when we were finally having a good time together again?"

But before Lisa could answer, Amy picked up her guitar and went into the other bedroom. A minute later, Palmer got up and followed her. "What I want to know," she complained as she went, "is whatever happened to the Foxes of the Third Dimension . . . the ones who used to be such good friends?"

CHAPTER TEN

———————⟡———————

Dear Mars,

Have you studied the Cold War yet in history class? Well, if you want a real-life lesson in what it was like, all you have to do is walk into Suite 3-D at Fox Hall! Lisa and I have to keep on living together, but we're hardly even speaking to each other anymore! As you can imagine, it's not very pleasant around here. I mean, even though I'm still really angry with Lisa, I didn't mean for it to be like this!

I guess the worst thing she's done is to call me a junior Kate Majors. That really hurt my feelings, and I just can't stop thinking about it. It's not that I don't like Kate—I do! She has a lot of wonderful traits, and she's been a very good friend to me. But I certainly don't want to be just like her! After all, she can be awfully bossy, and she's not very popular. I can't believe Lisa thinks I'm exactly like her!

Anyway, the good news is that my campaign platform is

really shaping up. I've been working on my final speech, and I'm proud of it so far. I wish you could be here to hear me deliver it—I need the moral support!

Write back soon,
Shanon

P.S. Your suggestion box suggestion was really excellent. Thanks!

Dear Lisa,

Hey, what's with you? Are you still there, or did you transfer to Brier Hall? I wrote you a letter a week and a half ago, and I haven't heard a word since.

Your lonely pen pal,
Rob

Lisa scanned Rob's letter, sighed guiltily, and then stuffed it into her pocket. She knew she should have answered his last letter, but she just hadn't had the time. She had been too busy electioneering to give much thought to Rob lately. And now she was way behind in her homework assignments, too! She would answer his letter tonight, she promised herself—just as soon as she finished writing her overdue history paper, filling in the missing pages in her science lab book, and studying for Friday's math test.

Lisa was too busy to write to Rob, but Mars and Shanon were continuing to write back and forth almost every day. And Mars's latest letter was the most exciting one yet!

Dear Shanon,

I have a surprise for you, and I absolutely positively have to see you so I can give it to you. Do you think you can get permission to go to town this coming Saturday afternoon? I know you'll be using up a town trip, but I don't think you'll regret it. If you could just happen to wander into Figaro's Pizza at about twelve-thirty, I'll make it worth your while.

Let me know ASAP,
Mars the Mysterious

The instant she'd finished reading Mars's letter, Shanon ran down to Miss Grayson's door and knocked.

"Come in," a pleasant voice responded.

"Hi, Miss Grayson," Shanon said as she walked into the cozy apartment. "Do you think I could possibly have a town pass for Saturday?"

"Going on a shopping spree?" Miss Grayson asked with a smile.

Shanon considered telling her about her date with Mars. After all, Miss Grayson had a boyfriend of her own—at least the girls were pretty sure that she and Mr. Griffith, the handsome young English teacher, were romantically involved. But Miss Grayson was already pulling out her record book and checking Shanon's name.

"Well, according to this, you still have two town trips left, Shanon," she said. "But you know the rules. You have to find another girl to go with you."

"No problem," Shanon said. "I'll let you know who it is as soon as I decide."

"That will be fine," Miss Grayson said, closing the record book. "How's the campaign going?" she asked. "I noticed one of your posters over at Booth Hall. The lettering was just beautiful—really eye-catching."

"Amy helped me with that one. She knows calligraphy."

"Well, be sure to tell her I think she did an excellent job!"

"I will!" Shanon promised. She said good-bye and hurried back toward her suite. On the way, she made up her mind to ask Amy to go to town with her. With a pang she realized that only a week or so ago she would have just assumed Lisa would be the one to go.

Every time she thought about Lisa, Shanon started to feel terrible, so she shook herself and tried to think about Mars instead. She went into the suite and found Amy idly strumming her guitar in the sitting room.

"Hey, Amy," Shanon exclaimed. "Mars has asked me to meet him in town Saturday. He says he has a surprise for me, but he wants to deliver it in person!"

Amy put down her guitar and grinned. "I'm glad something interesting is happening to someone around here!"

"Well, I need somebody to go with me on the town trip. Do you want to come?"

"Sure! I'd love to. Do you have any idea what the surprise could be?"

"Not a clue," Shanon said. "All I know is that we're supposed to just *happen* to be in Figaro's at twelve-thirty."

"Well, I'm always more than happy to go to Figaro's," Amy laughed.

"Great," Shanon said. "Then it's settled." She glanced at her watch and made a face. "I have to hurry over to the library now," she said. "The librarian is holding a book I need for my history paper; and if I don't claim it right now, somebody else might take it out."

"Okay, Shanon. See you later."

As Shanon hurried out into the hallway, Lisa quietly closed the bedroom door and flopped down on her bed. She didn't exactly mean to eavesdrop on Amy and Shanon's conversation, but she couldn't help overhearing. And now she was sorry she did.

How could Shanon have asked *Amy* to go to town with her? Shanon and Lisa always went everywhere together. Just because they'd had one little fight, it didn't mean they were supposed to start hanging around with other people all the time!

Lisa got up again and started pacing around the bedroom. It was pretty clear that Amy's loyalties were shifting toward Shanon. Amy might have nominated Lisa, but that didn't seem to mean much to her now. She was always going on about Shanon's good ideas, Shanon's hard work, Shanon this, Shanon that! Lisa was positive she had even recognized Amy's calligraphy on one of Shanon's campaign posters. Amy, that traitor, was probably already planning to vote for Shanon!

And as for Palmer, she was no better. She hardly even

seemed to know there was a campaign going on! All she did was moon around about Sam O'Leary, hoping and praying he'd ask her out on a date! She was no help at all these days.

Lisa stopped pacing in front of her bureau and turned to face herself in the mirror. "Who needs them?" she said out loud. "This is Lisa McGreevy we're talking about here! Even if my own suitemates don't care about me, I'm still one of the most popular third-formers in the school! There are lots of other girls in Fox Hall who'll be glad to vote for me!"

She glanced at the clock on her nightstand and saw that there was still about a half hour to go before dinnertime. She decided to get to the dining hall early, so she'd have a chance to talk to more people before they ate. She ran a brush through her hair and then walked purposefully out of the room.

Fifteen minutes later, when Amy and Shanon walked into the dining hall, they saw Lisa sitting at a table in the far corner of the room, laughing and talking with a whole table of third-formers.

"Wow!" Amy exclaimed. "Look at Lisa over there with that group from New York who always hang out together. Those girls are so tight with each other, they hardly even speak to anybody else! I didn't know Lisa was friends with them."

"She probably wasn't until a few minutes ago," Shanon said ruefully. "You know how Lisa is. She has that way of sitting down in a group and suddenly making everybody notice her. I'd be way too shy to ever do anything like that!"

"So would most people!" Amy laughed. "But *shy* isn't a word anybody would ever use to describe Lisa!"

"No, they wouldn't," Shanon agreed. She took a bite of the leg of lamb Mrs. Butter had made for dinner that night. Then she stared over at Lisa again and said, "What in the world is she doing *now*?"

Amy looked up from her forkful of roast potatoes. "It looks like she's picking up her plate," she said, glancing across the room. "She's going over to another table and sitting down with those girls from the fourth floor."

Shanon blinked as she realized what Lisa was doing. "I guess she's on the campaign trail," she said unhappily. Suddenly, her mouthful of lamb tasted dry and chewy. "She's out there collecting all the votes she can! What chance do I have against somebody who can do that?"

Amy patted Shanon's hand. "Don't worry about it," she said. "I think you might be surprised at how many girls have gotten to know who you are and are listening to your ideas lately. I don't think Lisa has this election locked up *at all*!"

"I hope you're right," Shanon said miserably. "Because if talking to people is the way to get votes, Lisa's going to beat me by a landslide!"

CHAPTER ELEVEN

On Saturday morning, Lisa asked Palmer to come into her bedroom for a few minutes. "You know a lot about clothes, Palmer," she said. "I'm trying to figure out what I should wear the night I give my campaign speech."

"But, Lisa," Palmer said, "I've already been through your entire wardrobe with you twice this week. I thought you'd decided on the bright blue dress with the silver butterflies on it. You said it would really get everybody's attention."

"I know I did," Lisa said as she yanked some other clothes out of her closet. "But now I'm afraid that dress might be too outrageous. I mean, I don't want it to be obvious that I'm trying to get attention."

"All right," Palmer said, settling down on the edge of Lisa's bed. "Show me what else you're considering."

She watched patiently as Lisa held up a dark green silk blouse and matching loose-fitting trousers in one hand and a deep red shirt dress in the other. "If you're going for subtle," Palmer advised, "the green is better." She stood up to leave, but Lisa waved her back down.

"Just one more minute," Lisa said. "What about these?" She picked up a yellow and black checkered sweatshirt and a pair of black velour pants. "Or do you think maybe I should just wear my jeans?"

"I still like the silk pants and top," Palmer said. She got to her feet. "And now I've got to go write another letter to Sam. Have you finished your campaign speech yet?"

"Not yet," Lisa said absentmindedly as she pulled a sequined T-shirt out of her bottom drawer. "I'm not sure I'll actually bother writing anything down. I might just get up there and wing it."

Palmer stared at her. "But wouldn't you be nervous—standing up in front of everybody like that without knowing what you're going to say?"

"Oh, no. I never get nervous in front of people. If there's one thing I know how to do, it's talk! Besides, just looking at my competition gives me all the confidence I need. Shanon and Muffin will both probably fall to pieces and start crying or fainting the minute they have to open their mouths!" She reached into her closet and pulled out a pinstriped jumpsuit. "Palmer, what if I wore this with my red leather belt and red cowboy boots?" she asked.

But Palmer, who normally could talk about clothes for hours on end, had already escaped to the sitting room. There she found Shanon, brushing her hair in front of the mirror.

It was almost time for her to go meet Mars, and she was tentatively experimenting with different hairstyles for the trip.

"Why don't you just wear it hanging down around your shoulders like that?" Palmer suggested. "It makes you look really glamorous, like Christie Brinkley."

Shanon stared at her reflection in the mirror. Then she smiled. "No, I don't think it's really me," she said. "You're the only one who looks like a model around here, Palmer. I guess I'm destined to wear my plain old braid forever!" She pulled her hair behind her ears and rapidly rebraided it.

Just then Amy came into the room. As usual, she was dressed mostly in black—this time, a long silver and black U-2 T-shirt and shiny bike pants. Her hair was moussed up into pointy spikes around her head. "Ready to go, Shanon?" she asked.

Shanon glanced down at her own outfit and shrugged. Normally, for such a special occasion, she would have borrowed something more dramatic from Lisa's huge wardrobe. But today she put on her own plain tan slacks and a brown and white striped shirt. "I guess I'm as ready as I'll ever be," she said.

"Wait a minute," Amy said. She ran into her bedroom and hurried back out with a brightly colored patchwork cotton vest. "My parents got this for me the last time they were in China," she said. "I haven't worn it before because it's too big, but it would really look great on you."

Shanon put the vest on over her shirt and glanced at her

69

reflection in the mirror. What she saw brought a smile to her face. The Chinese vest had transformed her boring outfit into something exotic and unusual. It did look great!

"Thanks, Amy," she said.

"Thank my mom and dad." Amy laughed. "And now we'd better get going or Mars will really be in orbit."

Half an hour later, the two girls parked their bikes outside Figaro's and went inside. Mars was already sitting at a booth waiting for them.

"Hi, Shanon! Hi, Amy!" he called. "I ordered a Monstro with extra cheese, plus a round of colas. I hope that's okay."

"It's fantastic," Amy said. "I'm so hungry I could eat the whole thing myself!"

"Me too," Shanon said quietly. She struggled to think of something else to say; but as usual when she hadn't seen Mars for a while, she felt terribly tongue-tied.

Mars turned to look at her. "That's a fantastic vest you're wearing, Shanon," he said.

"It's Amy's," she explained. "Her parents got it in China."

"Well, it may be Amy's, but it could have been made for you. The green patches are the exact same color as your eyes."

Shanon's face turned red, and Amy cleared her throat. "Hey! Here comes the pizza!" Amy said. She grabbed two pieces and hurriedly wolfed them down with her soda. Then she glanced at her watch. "Whoa!" she exclaimed. "If I don't go to the record store right now, I won't have any time there at all." She took a quick wipe at her mouth with a paper napkin and slid out of the booth. "I'll meet you back here in twenty minutes. Okay, Shanon?"

"Okay," Shanon said.

She and Mars watched Amy leave. Then they turned back toward each other and smiled. "Good old Amy," Mars said. "She really knows when to make an exit!"

Shanon felt her cheeks growing hot again, and she quickly grabbed her drink to give herself something to do. Mars took another bite of pizza. Then he picked up a brown paper bag on the seat next to him.

"Here's the surprise I told you about," he said, handing the bag to Shanon. "I hope you like it better than your birthday surprise!"

Shanon peered into the bag and gasped. "Campaign buttons!" She reached inside and pulled out one of the buttons. On the front of it was a cartoon picture of a grinning fox with long eyelashes and a big smile. A speech bubble was coming out of her mouth. Inside the bubble it read "Shanon Davis for Student Council!"

"This is fantastic!" Shanon cried. "Thank you, Mars! How did you ever think of such a thing?"

"I got the idea when I saw one of those little machines for making the buttons advertised in a catalogue. I drew the picture myself. The fox is for Fox Hall—*and* the Foxes of the Third Dimension! Get it?"

"I get it—and so will everybody else at school! It's perfect." She pinned one of the buttons onto her shirt. "These

71

buttons are going to make me feel much more confident about this whole thing!"

"So you're still feeling nervous?"

"A little," Shanon admitted. Then she made a face. "Better make that a lot! Particularly about standing up in front of everyone and giving a speech. I'm sure I'll start stuttering and forget what I have to say."

"No, you won't," Mars said. "Because I know what you're like. You'll practice your speech so many times, you'll know it backward and forward. I'm sure you won't leave out a single word." He leaned over and patted her hand, and Shanon's heart did a flip-flop. "The important thing to remember," Mars went on, "is to try to be a big-mouth, like me."

Shanon giggled, and Mars shook his head. "Better yet," he said, "be *yourself*! Just remember to talk loudly—project your voice so that it reaches the people sitting in the back row."

"I wish you were going to be there," Shanon said. "Though you might feel a little odd being the only boy in a room full of girls!"

"I think I could handle it." Mars grinned. "Anyway, you know I'll be thinking about you, wherever I am."

Shanon smiled and blushed again as she suddenly realized Mars had never taken his hand away from hers! Ten minutes later, when Amy came back from the record store, the two of them were still sitting in the booth, holding hands and listening to an old Beatles song on the jukebox.

Amy came up to the table and cleared her throat. Shanon and Mars both jumped and quickly dropped hands. "We'd better get going, Shanon," Amy began. Then she saw Shanon's button and gave a little shriek. "Shanon! Where did you get that button? It's totally excellent!"

Shanon nodded in Mars's direction. "Mars designed it," she said proudly. She pointed at the paper bag. "And he made a whole bunch of them for the campaign."

Amy took a button out of the bag and studied the picture. "This fox is really rad!" she said. "A totally fresh visual pun." And without thinking, she pinned the button to her T-shirt. Still standing, she said, "Come on, Shanon. We only have twenty minutes to ride all the way back to school before we get thrown in the dungeon for being late. 'Bye, Mars! Catch you later!"

"Good-bye, Mars," Shanon said, sliding out of the booth. "And thanks again for the buttons."

"Good luck with the election, Shanon," he said. "Write me a letter soon." He gave her a little wink, and her heart did another flip-flop. She couldn't wait to tell Lisa that she and Mars had actually held hands! But all at once she felt a pang as she remembered that she and Lisa weren't even speaking to each other anymore. She couldn't tell her about Mars! She'd have to settle for writing a letter to her sister Doreen instead.

Shanon and Amy made it back to school with time to spare. As soon as they walked into the suite, Palmer asked Shanon how her date with Mars had gone.

"Well, it wasn't exactly a date," Shanon said. "He just wanted to give me these." She went over to Palmer's chair and showed her one of the campaign buttons. As she did, Lisa came into the room. She took a quick look at the buttons but didn't comment on them.

"These are really super, Shanon," Palmer said. "This fox looks as if it was drawn by a professional artist!" She turned the button over and looked at the back. "Mars must have gone to a lot of trouble to make all these. He must *really* like you!"

Shanon smiled and blushed. "I guess so," she agreed. "He kind of acted like he did today!"

"Kind of?" Amy cried. "I thought the two of you looked pretty cozy when I came back from the record store! Exactly what went on while I was gone anyway? Spill it, Shanon! We want all the details."

Amy and Palmer both perched on the sofa and eagerly waited to hear Shanon's story, but Lisa quietly slipped away into the bedroom. It was bad enough that Shanon was barely speaking to her. But now Amy and Palmer were clearly on Shanon's side. And, to top it all off, Mars seemed really involved with her campaign. Those buttons were totally wild. It just wasn't fair.

Lisa sat down at the desk and pulled out a piece of stationery and a pen.

Dear Rob,
I haven't heard from you for a while, and I guess it's

74

probably my turn to write. This campaign has really been keeping me busy lately. Shanon's spending a lot of time on it, too—and she's not the only one! Your roommate Mars is helping her out! You should see the campaign buttons he made for her. They're really great!

I was wondering if you could think of something like that to help me out—not that I think Shanon might actually beat me or anything!—but I just know the girls in the dorm are all going to die over those buttons!

Please let me know if you have any ideas,
Lisa

For the next several days, Lisa eagerly checked her mailbox every morning and afternoon, but it was always empty. At last she decided she would have to come up with her own campaign gimmick. As she had predicted in her letter to Rob, all the girls had loved Shanon's buttons, particularly when they heard that her Ardsley pen pal had made them. But Lisa couldn't think of any good way of attracting attention to her own campaign, and she started to feel slightly desperate. Finally, though, an idea came to her as she was leafing through some old comic books in the common room. She snatched up one of the comics and raced out of the dorm and over to the art center. There she found a giant piece of poster board and some brightly colored acrylic paints. Using one of the comic book characters as a model, she painted a giant picture of herself dressed as a ninja warrior with her hand raised in a clenched fist. In the lower left-hand corner of the poster, she painted two tiny mice cowering behind a school desk. One of the mice had a long braid, and the other was holding a little muffin. A speech balloon coming out of one mouse's mouth said, "Take me to your leader? No way!"

Across the top of the poster, Lisa painted the words: LISA MCGREEVY FOR STUDENT COUNCIL! When she was finished, she looked at her artwork and laughed out loud. Even if she did say so herself, it was a pretty funny poster. And it was sure to be noticed.

Before the paint was even dry, Lisa dragged the poster out of the art room and over to Booth Hall, where she tacked it up on the bulletin board. Then, still chuckling to herself, she headed for the library to do her homework.

About an hour later, Kate Majors came banging on the door to Suite 3-D. When Shanon called, "Come in," Kate stuck her head inside and motioned for Shanon to come with her.

"You're not going to believe this," Kate said, practically dragging Shanon down the hall and out of the dorm. "She's hit a new low."

"Believe what?" Shanon asked in confusion as she followed Kate along the sidewalk. "Who's hit a new low? What and whom are you talking about?"

"The *whom* I'm talking about is Lisa McGreevy. And the *what* . . . is *this!*" By then the two girls had entered Booth Hall and come to a stop in front of the bulletin board. Kate pointed an accusing finger at Lisa's poster.

Shanon stared at it for a minute. At her first sight of the ninja warrior, she started to smile. But when she noticed the two little mice in the corner, she gasped in horror. "One of them has a muffin!" she cried. "And the other one has a braid! Lisa is calling Muffin and me a pair of scared little *mice*! I just can't believe it!"

"You'd better believe it!" Kate said. "And you'd better do something about it."

"But . . . what can I do? Draw a mean poster myself?"

"No. That would be stooping to Lisa's level. I have a better idea. But we've got to start working on it right now." She grabbed Shanon's arm and hauled her down the hall toward the school newspaper office.

Two days later, a special election edition of the Alma Stephens *Ledger* was published. Most of the front page was taken up by an interview with Shanon Davis, outlining some of her ideas for improving dorm life at Fox Hall and concluding with the statement: "I think voters should look very closely at the kind of campaign each candidate is conducting. If a girl is waging a mean, low-down campaign now, what kind of dorm rep will she be in the future?"

The instant Lisa finished reading the story, she stormed into the suite and slapped the newspaper down on the desk where Shanon was working. "How could you do this?" she demanded. "How could you and your buddy Kate use the school newspaper to your own advantage? If *The New York Times* did this, somebody would slap them with a lawsuit in a minute!"

"Newspapers endorse political candidates all the time," Shanon said uncomfortably.

"Not when the candidate and her campaign manager both work for the paper, they don't! I believe it's called *conflict of interest*! This isn't fair, and you know it. Besides that, it's just plain nasty! Even though you don't say my name in this story, everybody will know you're talking about me! You make me sound like some kind of criminal! I can't believe you'd do something this mean, Shanon!"

Shanon pushed back her chair and got to her feet. Her face was flushed, and she had to blink rapidly to keep back the tears that had suddenly filled her eyes. "Mean?" Shanon cried. "*You're* calling *me* mean? After you drew that horrible poster showing me and Muffin as chicken-livered little mice and yourself as some kind of kung-fu heroine? You've got to be kidding, Lisa. When it comes to meanness, you're so well qualified, you could earn a black belt in it!"

CHAPTER TWELVE

When Amy came into Suite 3-D that afternoon, she found all the curtains drawn and the lights turned off, even though it was only four o'clock. As she reached for the light switch, a voice cried out, "Don't do that!" It was Palmer. "Dawn is reading my palm, and the atmosphere has to be just right," she went on more calmly.

"Dawn?" Amy came into the room and peered around. Palmer was huddled in the corner with a tall, thin girl, who was wearing a red fringed shawl over an ankle-length black dress. Amy recognized her as Dawn Hubbard, a fourth-former she had seen around the halls between classes. Dawn had long, perfectly straight black hair and enormous black eyes. Amy had always thought she was a little weird, but she'd never realized just *how* weird!

"Palmer," Amy began, "I need to have the lights on so I can find my running shoes and—"

"Silence!" Dawn ordered. "I have to concentrate!" She turned on a tiny penlight and pointed it at Palmer's outstretched palm. Amy sighed and sank down in a chair to wait.

"Hmmmm," said Dawn. "I see a boat ride here . . . but the waters are full of danger and turbulence!"

"Oh, no!" Palmer gasped. "*How* dangerous? Am I going to drown?"

"No. No, I don't think so. I see protection and safety . . . in the arms of a handsome stranger!"

"That's more like it," Palmer said happily. "Who is he?"

"How should I know?" Dawn asked. "I'm reading your palm, not the telephone directory!" She snapped off the flashlight, flicked the wall switch back on, and removed her shawl with a flourish.

"Is that it?" Palmer asked. "That's all you can see in my palm?"

"For now," Dawn answered, heading for the door. "I've got to meet my roommate at the snack bar in five minutes. Let me know if I'm right!" she called back.

"Thanks, Dawn! I will!"

Just as Dawn left, Lisa walked into the room, still in a terrible mood from her fight with Shanon. As she closed the door behind her, she asked, "Who in the world was that?"

"Dawn Hubbard," Palmer said excitedly. "She just read my palm! She said I'm going to have a boat ride on dangerous waters, but I'll find safety with a handsome stranger! I'm pretty sure the stranger would have to be Sam—I just can't figure out how in the world he and I will ever end up on a boat together!"

Lisa laughed loudly. "Oh, give me a break, Palmer! How can you take any of that stuff seriously? How could Dawn Hubbard possibly be able to predict your future by staring at your hand for a few minutes? It's just a lot of nonsense!"

Palmer put her hands on her hips. "I don't think it's nonsense at all!" she said indignantly. "Palm reading is an ancient art. And, besides, what's wrong with it? I like imagining that Sam and I might meet on a boat somewhere. Maybe it'll be on an ocean liner or maybe on a rowboat, but I don't care! It's just fun to hope it might happen one day!"

"You can hope all you want," Lisa said, "but I still say it's ridiculous."

"Well, maybe it is," Palmer said, shrugging. "But—"

"Oh, don't listen to Lisa," Amy interrupted Palmer. "She's just jealous 'cause there's no handsome stranger in her future."

Lisa whirled around and stared at Amy in amazement. "Don't tell me you believe in this palm-reading stuff, too!" she asked.

"That's not the point! The point is that Palmer was enjoying herself until you came in and started making fun of the whole thing. I just don't think that's very nice!"

Lisa's eyes narrowed as she looked back and forth between Amy and Palmer. "I guess I'm finally beginning to get the message around here," she said. "You two are coming through loud and clear."

"What are you talking about, Lisa?" Amy asked.

"You know perfectly well, Amy! I'm saying that I've finally realized exactly where this suite stands!"

"Well, if you're talking about the election," Amy said, "you've realized wrong. I haven't decided who I'm voting for yet. And even if I had, I'm not sure I'd tell you. It *is* going to be a secret ballot, you know."

Although she knew she'd been asking for it, Lisa was stung by Amy's response. She had been counting on Amy's vote. And suddenly she was sure that it was going to Shanon!

Lisa turned from Amy to Palmer. "What about you, Palmer? Are you voting for Shanon, too?"

"That's none of your business," Palmer said airily.

"What do you mean it's none of my business? I'm one of the candidates! Of course it's my business! And I think you've already made up your mind to vote for Shanon!"

"You can think what you want," Palmer huffed as she headed toward her bedroom, "but I'm still not telling you how I'm planning to vote." She turned around and faced Lisa again. "I will say one thing, though. I can't *wait* until this horrible election is over with so we can have some peace and quiet around here again!"

CHAPTER THIRTEEN

"Mail call," Shanon said, entering the suite with a handful of letters. "Everybody report to the sitting room for your letters!" she announced cheerfully.

Both bedroom doors opened as Amy, Palmer, and Lisa came out to claim their mail. Shanon had already read her own letter from Mars on the way to the dorm, and it was such a nice one she offered to show it to the other girls. "I'll read it out loud," she announced, "the way we used to when we first started writing to The Unknown."

Dear Shanon,
You must be getting pretty excited about the election. I know you're going to be just fine on your own, but I couldn't resist sending you some ideas for jokes you can use in your campaign speech. You could start out by saying, "A funny thing happened to me on the way to this meeting tonight. I

saw a boy, and I didn't turn into a pumpkin!" Then you could suggest that Alma Stephens turn co-ed! (Which I think is a terrific idea since all they'd have to do is merge with Ardsley!) You could also do some "cross" jokes—like what do you get if you cross Miss Pryn with your pet dog? Answer: A cocker spaniel that bites your head off! On second thought . . . maybe you'd better not use that one, you might get in trouble. Maybe you could use: What do you get if you cross Miss Grayson with a traffic signal? Answer: A light that turns red every time it sees Mr. Griffith! But, then again, maybe not!

As you can see, with Mars around the fun never stops. Just let me know if you need more material.

The Johnny Carson of Ardsley,
Mars Martinez

P.S. I'm still thinking about how much fun it was seeing you at Figaro's. I wish we could do it every Saturday!

By the time Shanon finished reading Mars's letter, all the girls were laughing—even Lisa. They were still giggling as they ripped open their own letters and read them to themselves.

"Oh my gosh, oh my gosh!" Palmer screamed when she'd finished hers. "I'm simply going to die right here on this spot!"

"So am I." Lisa groaned. She crumpled her letter into a ball, tossed it in the waste basket, and started walking

84

toward her bedroom. "I give up!" she said. "This pen pal business is the pits!"

"My letter's pretty bad, too." Amy sighed. Like Lisa, she turned around and headed toward her bedroom.

"I don't believe this!" Palmer said plaintively. "How can you *do* this to me?"

Amy and Lisa stopped in their tracks and stared at Palmer in surprise. "Do what, Palmer?" Shanon asked. "Is something wrong? You look upset."

"I *am* upset!" Palmer sniffed. "Amy and Lisa sound like they're ready to give up on their pen pals, just when things are getting started with mine! It's not fair. Lisa was the one who thought up the pen pal idea—and now she wants to forget the whole thing."

"I have my reasons," Lisa mumbled. "Wait till you read my letter." She fished it out of the trash and handed it to Palmer, who smoothed it out and then began reading aloud:

Dear Lisa,

You have some nerve! You don't answer my last two letters, and then out of the blue you write and ask me for ideas about your campaign—as if you're the only person in the world or something! Well, other people have problems too, you know. I already told you I was worried about my schoolwork and my track coach. But do you even mention them? No! All you do is talk about yourself! Maybe I shouldn't be surprised that you don't say a thing about my problems! You're probably much too busy with your po-

litical career to even bother reading my letters these days!
Maybe you don't even want a pen pal anymore. I'm not at
all sure I do!

    Anyway, if you don't have time to answer, don't bother!

Rob

"Wow!" Palmer exclaimed when she finished reading. "Rob's really steamed."

"Yeah," Amy said in agreement. "That's pretty extreme. But at least he's still interested enough to get mad at you, Lisa. Wait till you hear John's letter!"

Dear Amy,
    Hi. How are things at Alma? Everything's the same at Ardsley.

John

"Go ahead and read the rest of it," Palmer urged.

"That's it," Amy said ruefully. "That's all he wrote! And come to think of it, that's pretty much all I wrote to *him* in my last letter! We don't seem to have much to say to each other anymore!"

"Well, I don't believe this is happening!" Palmer wailed. "From what I can tell, Lisa and Amy have just about ruined their relationships with their pen pals. And here I am with a really juicy letter from Sam, and nobody even wants to hear it! What's happening to the pen pals? What's happen-

86

ing to us? All year the three of you have been telling me how special we are, how we have to stick together, have to help each other out. But now it seems like that's the exact opposite of what's going on! Are we still the Foxes of the Third Dimension, or are we just a plain old bunch of girls who just happened to get stuck rooming together for a year?"

For a long moment, the room was completely silent as the other girls thought about what Palmer had said. Lisa was the first to speak. "You're right, Palmer," she said. But it was Shanon she was looking at. "We *have* all been acting like enemies lately."

"And selfish ones, too," Shanon chimed in. "Sorry, Palmer," she said, looking right at Lisa.

"Well, all right," Lisa said. "Let's put our heads together the way we used to. First of all, Amy, I'm sure we can help you solve your problem with John. It seems to me that the two of you got into a rut writing each other about your songs and poems all the time. Maybe you should try writing to him about something else—and I don't mean the weather!"

"But what?" Amy asked. "I can't think of anything interesting."

"Why don't you just tell him about yourself?" Palmer suggested. "When I first started writing to Sam, that's what you told me to do."

"But what *about* myself?" Amy asked.

"Oh, anything," Palmer said. "Your ideas, your interests, what you've been doing, what you've been thinking about."

Amy fiddled with the single copper hoop in her ear. "Well,

I guess I could try it," she said slowly. "But what if John thinks I'm boring?"

Lisa, Shanon, and Palmer all burst out laughing. "Amy," Lisa said, "if there's one thing you are *not,* it's boring!"

"That's for sure!" Shanon agreed. "If you just wrote John about what you're wearing right now, he'd probably think it was fascinating!"

Amy looked down at herself and giggled. She'd been running by the river that afternoon, and she had on an outfit inspired by one of her idols, track star Florence Griffith Joyner: an orange and black tiger-striped spandex leotard, with one leg encased in silver-spangled tights and the other one bare!

"Okay," Amy said. "I get your point. I'll write John all about myself and see what happens." She glanced over at Lisa. "But what are we going to do about Lisa's problem with Rob?"

"I have an idea about that," Shanon said. "Since it's pretty obvious you've hurt his feelings, Lisa, I think the first thing you have to do is write back to him and apologize."

"Shanon's right, Lisa," Amy said. "He sounds pretty upset about your not answering his letters."

"I guess he has a right to be," Lisa admitted. "First I didn't even bother to answer his letters. And then when I finally did write him, I only talked about myself—and I asked him for a favor on top of it!"

"I think you'd better throw yourself at his mercy," Palmer said. "Apologize all over the place, and tell him how much you like being his pen pal. That way, he'll stop worrying that you don't like him anymore!"

"Good idea," Lisa said with a smile. "I feel better already. I'm going to go write Rob a letter right now!"

"Oh, no, you don't," Palmer cried. "We've solved all your problems, but you guys *still* haven't heard my letter from Sam!"

"Sorry, Palmer," Amy said. "We're all ears. Fire away."

Dear Palmer,

I've got only one thing to say about your last letter, and that is "Wow!" Every time I hear from you, it makes me wish I had a chance to see you. At first I thought it would never happen. But now I've come up with a Plan!

Palmer glanced up from the letter and looked around at the other girls. She definitely had their attention now.

"Go on, Palmer!" Amy said impatiently. "Let's hear his plan!"

"I just wanted to be sure you're all really interested," Palmer said, batting her big blue eyes. "If I'm boring you . . ."

"Palmer!" Lisa yelled. "You've made your point. We're sorry we didn't beg to hear the letter before. But now we're dying to hear the rest of it—so read it or we'll tackle you and take it!"

"Okay, okay!" Palmer laughed. She picked up the letter and started reading again.

89

It turns out my school is going to have a Spring Fair as a fundraiser for the library. I didn't say anything about it before because I was afraid you'd think it was pretty rinky-dink stuff. But a few days ago I heard they're planning to make it a really Big Deal, importing a professional traveling carnival with games and rides and even a Ferris wheel! I'm not promising you Disney World or anything, but it should be lots of fun.

Now for the bottom line. The fair is scheduled for next Saturday night. Do you think there's any way you could get permission to go with me? I'd like to show you off to everybody at school. Let me know as soon as you can!

Sam

"Palmer!" Amy squealed. "Your fantasy dream came true! Sam asked you for a date!"

Palmer got to her feet and started jumping around. "I know, I know, I know!" she cried. "Isn't it unbelievable?"

All at once, her blue eyes clouded. "But what if I can't go? I mean, I can't imagine Miss Grayson letting me go into town by myself to meet a *boy*. We're not even allowed to go shopping alone!"

Shanon chewed on the end of her braid. "Hmmmm," she said thoughtfully. "I just might be able to help you out with this. Sam said the fair was supposed to be a fundraiser for the Brighton town library, right?"

Palmer looked down at Sam's letter again. "Uh-huh," she said. "He did say that."

"Well, you know my family lives right in Brighton, too. And it just so happens that my mother does a lot of volunteer work for the library. If I remember right, she told me they were going to have a used-book sale at the fair."

"That's great, Shanon," Palmer said. "I think your mom is a wonderful person. But how does that help me get to go on my date with Sam?"

"I'm not sure," Shanon said. "But there's got to be some way we can use the connection!"

"How about this?" Lisa said. "What if Shanon gets her mother to ask Miss Pryn to send an Alma volunteer—like that adorable Amy Ho, for instance—into town for the fair so she can help at the used-book booth?"

"And adorable Amy Ho just happens to ask if she can bring a friend along," Amy continued.

"And the friend just happens to be me!" Palmer cried ecstatically. "It's perfect!"

"It *is* perfect!" Shanon said happily. "In fact, I bet Miss Pryn will love it. She's always saying the school should have a better relationship with the townspeople. And Amy, it would actually be fun selling books to all the local kids."

"There's only one problem," Palmer said, her smile fading at the thought. "If I'm stuck at the booth all night, how will I get to see Sam?"

"Oh, I'm sure my mother won't mind if you take a break," Shanon said. "A nice long one. She's pretty understanding about that type of thing."

"Fantastic!" Amy exclaimed triumphantly, jumping to

her feet. "The Foxes live! We've solved all our problems in one fell swoop. Now, isn't this a lot more fun than squabbling about a stupid old election?"

The instant the words were out of her mouth, the room fell silent again. Amy bit her lip. She could have kicked herself for mentioning the election just when they had finally started acting like their old selves. She looked around the room at the tense faces. Oh, what was the use, anyway? she asked herself. She might as well face facts. They were *never* going to get along again—not until Lisa and Shanon stopped competing with each other!

CHAPTER FOURTEEN

Election night finally arrived. Suite 3-D was in an uproar. Lisa had spent the better part of the day still seeking the perfect outfit to wear for her speech. She finally settled on a pair of faded blue jeans with enormous holes in the knees, along with a wildly striped metallic T-shirt. She washed her hair and blew it dry so that it hung straight down her back. Then she added a pair of dangling silver earrings.

Shanon wore the same pair of tan slacks she'd worn for her meeting with Mars, along with Amy's quilted Chinese vest. Once again, she considered wearing her hair in several different styles, but ended up putting it back into her usual braid. *What they see is what they get,* she told her reflection in the mirror. Tonight was not the night to start pretending to be somebody she wasn't!

When it was time for the speeches, all the third-formers from Fox Hall gathered in the common room. As dorm monitor, Kate Majors chaired the meeting. She introduced the three candidates, and then announced that Muffin Talbot would speak first. There was some scattered applause as Muffin stood up and walked to the front of the room. "Good evening, fellow third-formers," she began in a soft, shaky voice. As she went on with her speech a few people in the front row started nodding and looking impressed. But it soon became obvious that no one else in the room could hear a word she was saying!

Most of the girls weren't even sure when Muffin's speech was over. But when the people in the front row started clapping, everyone else joined in. Then Kate introduced the next candidate, Lisa McGreevy.

Lisa surprised everybody by running to the front of the room, jumping up on a chair, and raising her clenched fist high into the air.

"Third-formers, unite!" she cried. "It's time we stopped getting such a raw deal at Alma Stephens!" She looked out at the audience, expecting the girls to start cheering and stomping their feet in response. But all she heard was an embarrassing silence. Everyone seemed stunned with surprise. Blushing furiously, she swallowed hard and climbed down from her chair.

"You ask what I mean by that!" she went on. "Well, what I mean is this. . . . Uh . . . it's not easy being a third-former! We're new to the school, and uh . . . that can be hard! And the older girls think they can boss us all around! And that's not fair! So that's why we need somebody to represent this dorm . . . somebody who can . . . uh . . . stand up for your rights! And I say that Lisa McGreevy is that somebody!"

She finished her speech with a dramatic bow. Once again, she seemed to be expecting a wild outburst, but she had to settle for some polite applause.

Finally, Shanon's turn came. She took a deep breath and walked up to the front of the room. Then she looked at the back row of the audience and tried to imagine Mars there, sitting next to the girls, silently encouraging her. She smiled and started to speak.

"I have to agree with my opponent about one thing," she said in a surprisingly loud, clear voice. "It isn't always easy being a third-former at a place like Alma Stephens. But instead of complaining about how bad things are, I think we should try to do something about it!

"I remember how lonely and lost I felt my first few days here. And, during the first week or so, the school did have a few 'orientation' events to help us deal with that kind of thing. But a new girl's problems don't stop at the end of the first week of school! I'd like to see more 'third-form only' activities throughout the year. The seniors have a pancake breakfast—I say, why can't we have a spaghetti dinner—or even better, how about an ice-cream sundae night?"

At that point, Shanon was interrupted by loud applause and shouts of approval. She grinned and went on with her speech. "And what about more co-ed activities with Ardsley?" she asked. Once again, she was interrupted as the audience voiced its agreement. "Of course, we'd all like to see more dances and social events. . . ." She stopped and motioned for silence. "But why can't the two schools do other things together? For instance, why can't some of us take classes over there sometimes—and learn about things that aren't taught here? I'd love to see their auto mechanics shop! And why can't Ardsley students come here for some of our classes? If you ask me, most of those guys could stand to learn a few things about home economics. Nowadays, men have to take part in running the home, too! Alma Stephens needs to keep pace with the real world!"

Shanon continued on in a clear voice that became more confident as she spoke. As she finished her speech, she looked out over the audience. They were quiet now, listening intently to everything she had to say. And then they were clapping enthusiastically as Shanon thanked them for their attention and headed back to her seat.

Afterwards, while Kate passed out ballot forms, some of the other girls congratulated Shanon on her speech. But Shanon didn't feel like talking to anyone. She sank down into her chair and let out a long sigh of relief.

It was finally over! she thought thankfully. And it had gone better than she had ever dared hope. She could hardly wait to write Mars all about it. Just as soon as her trembling legs would hold her up again, she would go back to the suite and do just that!

Across the room, Lisa was also sitting in her chair. But she was feeling anything but relieved. Instead, her stomach was churning, and her cheeks were on fire. She felt embarrassed about her short, badly prepared speech and the way it had been received. She was sorry she hadn't spent more time working on it. In all honesty, she hadn't spent *any* time working on it—and that fact had clearly been obvious to everyone!

The whole experience wouldn't have been so bad, she told herself, if Shanon hadn't done such an incredible job on *her* speech. Who would have believed it? The instant Shanon stood up in front of the audience, she seemed to turn into a different person! Granted, she had worked very hard on her speech and had thought of lots of good ideas about the school. But the way she delivered her speech was unbelievable, too. She was so forceful, so passionate, so strong . . . in fact, Shanon exhibited all the traits that Lisa liked to believe *she* had!

Of course, Lisa tried to reassure herself, the fact that Shanon's speech was terrific didn't necessarily mean she would win the election. The speeches didn't count for everything. Lisa was a lot more popular, and her friends would probably still vote for her.

But Amy, who was in the process of filling out her ballot, was thinking just the opposite. Even though she still liked Lisa and considered her a close friend, she decided to vote for Shanon.

Up until now, Amy had tried to keep an open mind about the election. After all, she had nominated Lisa herself, and she felt some loyalty. But tonight the contrast between Lisa's and Shanon's speeches had just been too great. Shanon was obviously taking the election much more seriously than Lisa. And Amy believed that was probably the way Shanon would handle the job of dorm rep as well.

Later that night, after lights out, Shanon and Lisa lay quietly in their beds. Their room wasn't very big, but the two girls had grown so far apart that Shanon thought the Atlantic Ocean could have fit between them. Several times she opened her mouth to speak. She remembered the expression on Lisa's face while the other girls were busy voting in the common room, and she knew her roommate had really regretted her speech. Shanon felt sorry for Lisa and wished she could say something to make her feel a little better.

In the old days, before the election, the two of them had talked about anything and everything together. If one of them was upset or depressed, she would tell the other one all about it, and then they would both try to figure out what to do. But now things were different. Now they kept their problems and their thoughts to themselves—or else they told other people about them.

On her side of the room, Lisa was having similar thoughts. She really wanted to congratulate Shanon on her speech, but somehow she just couldn't make herself say the words. She felt as if she hardly knew Shanon anymore. She wondered if she would ever again make such a good friend. Then she realized she didn't really want to. She still wanted to be best friends with Shanon!

She pulled the cover up to her chin and told herself to stop worrying and go to sleep. But just then an upsetting thought came to her. Tomorrow they would find out the results of the balloting, and only one of them would be dorm rep! Would the loser ever be able to forgive the winner? Would things between them ever be the same again?

Lisa turned over on her back and sat up in the dark. "Shanon?" she whispered tentatively. "Are you asleep?"

"No," Shanon whispered back. "Did you want to say something?" She sat up in her bed and eagerly leaned forward.

"Uh . . . well, yes," Lisa began uncertainly. "That is . . . I wanted to say . . . I wanted to say, 'Good luck!' With the election, I mean!"

"Thanks," Shanon said in a small voice. "I wanted to say that to you, too." She waited for Lisa to say something else, but apparently that was it. With a sigh of disappointment, Shanon lay back down, closed her eyes, and tried to go to sleep.

CHAPTER FIFTEEN

A sign on the bulletin board outside the common room announced the news: *Shanon Davis is Fox Hall's new dorm rep. Congratulations, Shanon!* Miss Grayson must have put it there late the previous night.

Lisa was one of the first people to see the notice. She hadn't been able to sleep very well, so she got up early and went to check the board. As she stood staring at the sign, she felt stunned and upset. She had honestly never believed she might lose!

She also felt humiliated. In her heart, she knew it was probably her own fault that she lost. She had been so concerned about being popular and picking out the right outfit that she had barely given a thought to the real issues of the election. She hadn't come up with one single contribution she would have made as Fox Hall's rep. And everybody in the dorm knew it!

All at once, Lisa felt as if she would die of shame if she saw anybody she knew ever again. She whirled away from the bulletin board and raced down the hall, almost running right into Shanon, who was coming from the other direction.

Shanon stopped in her tracks and stared after Lisa. Shanon was on her way to check the bulletin board. Even though several girls had already told her she won, she just wanted to make sure it was official. Now she didn't have to check. The look on Lisa's face told her all she needed to know.

Suddenly, the pride and excitement Shanon had been feeling started to evaporate. As she watched Lisa run down the hall and out the door, Shanon had to fight the urge to cry. She found herself wondering if the election had been worth all this. So what if she proved to the whole school that Shanon Davis was a strong, passionate leader? She lost her best friend in the process!

That day, Lisa skipped all her classes. She didn't even show up in the dining room for lunch. When she wasn't there for dinner either, the other three friends began to worry. If Lisa didn't turn up by lights out, they would have to tell Miss Grayson.

Shanon was relieved when her roommate finally wandered into the room a few minutes after eight that night. "Where's everyone else?" Lisa asked, looking around for Amy and Palmer.

"How could you forget?" Shanon answered lightly. "Tonight's the night of the carnival at Sam's school. Amy and Palmer left right after dinner!"

"Oh, that's right," Lisa said, staring at a spot just over Shanon's head. "I did forget. And speaking of dinner, I seem to have forgotten about that, too. I think I'll order one of those new giant meatball sandwiches from Figaro's before I pass out from hunger!" she added, still not meeting Shanon's eyes.

"Order me one, too," said Shanon, closing her book with a bang. "With extra sauce!"

Half an hour later, both girls were biting into the enormous, sloppy sandwiches. For a while, they concentrated on chewing and wiping drips of tomato sauce off their chins. Lisa finally broke the silence.

"Your campaign speech was really good, Shanon," she said quietly. "And so were you. I mean, the way you gave the speech was good. If I hadn't been one of the candidates, I would have voted for you myself!"

"I would have voted for you, too!" Shanon said quickly. "I mean, after all, you're my best . . ." Her voice trailed off, and she stared down at the remains of her sandwich.

Lisa waited for Shanon to finish, but Shanon just took another bite of her sandwich.

"I'm really sorry about that mouse poster I drew," Lisa said after a minute. "It *was* mean, particularly after you'd been so upset about being called shy and everything."

"Oh, that," Shanon said, looking up again. "It was actually pretty funny."

"Well, you're the only one who thought so!" Lisa said ruefully. "*I* don't even think it's funny anymore. And it wasn't true either. You are definitely not a mouse!"

"Maybe not. But I know I was getting pretty snotty for a while there. Waiting up for you when you came back from the kitchen and threatening to turn you in like that.... I can't believe I did that! I acted like a little dictator!"

There was another minute of silence while both girls thought about how close they had come to breaking up their friendship.

"I'm sorry I've been so awful lately," Lisa said. "Calling you a junior Kate Majors was truly nasty. I only said it because I was jealous. But I don't have any right to stop you from being friends with her. You can be friends with anybody you want to!"

Shanon darted a sideways look at Lisa. "Does that include being friends with you again?"

"Of course it does!" Lisa said with a big smile. "If you want to be, that is."

"Of course I do!" Shanon exclaimed. She got up on her knees and reached over to give Lisa a big hug. Lisa hugged her in return. Then they both sat down on the floor again to finish their sandwiches and talk over everything that had happened since the campaign began.

CHAPTER SIXTEEN

Later that night, Shanon announced that she wanted to cut her hair. "I promised myself I'd do it when I turned thirteen," she confided to Lisa. "But I've been chickening out ever since. Tonight I finally feel brave enough to go for it."

"Then I'll help you!" Lisa said, jumping to her feet. She ran into the bedroom and came back with a brush, comb, and scissors. Then, while Shanon sat on a chair in front of the mirror, Lisa unbraided her roommate's yard-long hair and brushed it till it shone. "Are you sure you really want to do this, Shanon?" she said after a few minutes of brushing. "Your hair is so long and beautiful. I'm afraid to cut it!"

"Then I'll do it myself!" Shanon said. She picked up the scissors, reached around behind her head, and grabbed a fistful of hair.

"No!" Lisa cried out in alarm. "You can't see what you're

doing!" She drew a long breath and took the scissors. "You'd better let me."

Painstakingly, Lisa divided Shanon's hair into sections which she clipped up on top of her head. Then slowly and carefully she began snipping away at the bottom section. When she finished that, she moved on to the next. Shanon had so much hair it took Lisa close to an hour to do the cutting. But at last she finished and stood back to admire her work. Shanon's hair hung down in soft waves around her shoulders. Fluffy curls framed her face, emphasizing her large eyes. She looked like a different person.

Shanon stared at her reflection in the mirror. As she turned her head this way and that, her hair swung out around her face.

"It's fantastic, Lisa!" she cried at last. "I love it!"

"Thank goodness for that!" Lisa laughed in relief. "I was afraid you might hate it—and you'd be furious with me right after we just started being friends again!" She reached out and gave Shanon's hair a final brush. "If I say so myself, it *does* look fantastic! You look much older and more sophisticated!"

A few minutes later, Amy and Palmer came bursting through the door. They took one look at Shanon, and their mouths dropped open. They couldn't seem to stop exclaiming about the new haircut and how great she looked. Shanon finally had to insist they change the subject so she could hear all about Palmer and Sam.

"It was unbelievable!" Palmer said, rolling her eyes dramatically. "It actually happened on water just the way Dawn Hubbard said it would! The carnival had one of those little boat rides that went around a haunted castle, and that's what we went on! And then Sam saved me! You see, they had these scary-looking alligators in the water, so naturally I screamed, and—"

"Palmer," Lisa interrupted, "do you mean to say you were really scared of a mechanical alligator?"

"Well. . . ." Palmer smiled slyly. "I may have overreacted just a little. But Sam didn't seem to mind."

Everybody giggled. "Go on, Palmer," Amy urged. "Tell them what happened next."

"Well, when I saw the alligator and screamed, Sam naturally thought I was terrified—so he saved me *by putting his arm around my shoulders*! And he kept it there for the whole rest of the ride!"

"Wow!" Amy breathed. "A romantic boat ride, snuggled up with a handsome stranger. Dawn was right! But I guess you can't exactly call Sam a handsome stranger anymore. It sounds like you two got to know each other pretty well tonight!"

"You're right about that." Palmer laughed. "But even though he's not a stranger anymore, I definitely still think he's handsome!"

"I should go apologize to Dawn for making fun of her fortune-telling," Lisa said sheepishly. "Too bad I didn't ask her to read my palm. If I'd known what was going to happen in my future, I wouldn't have bothered running in the election!"

"Don't say that, Lisa!" Shanon protested. "You were a good candidate!"

"I agree," Amy said. "But even so, I hope the two of you don't plan to compete against each other anytime soon. It's been like living on a battlefield around here!"

"Right!" Palmer said. "I think from now on we should concentrate on things we can do *with* each other, not *against* each other. Things that are fun—like writing to our pen pals!"

"Or raiding the kitchen!" Amy said. "Shanon's mother had me working so hard at the book booth, I didn't get a chance to eat a single snack at the carnival!"

"Oh, I don't know about that," Lisa said, looking sideways at Shanon. "Haven't you heard, Amy? Kitchen raids are against the rules!"

"Don't worry about it!" Shanon laughed. "If I hadn't just pigged out on a meatball hero, I'd be the first to join you!"

"Great," Amy said happily. "We avoided a fight. I hope we can keep up this harmony. In fact, I think we should make a solemn vow never to disagree again."

"Good idea!" Shanon said. "I agree."

"And I hereby pledge never to disagree about anything ever again!" Lisa said, holding her right hand up only half jokingly.

"Me, too!" Amy and Palmer chorused. Just then, a few

tinny musical notes sounded outside the window. The girls stopped talking immediately and stared at each other.

"The ice cream truck!" they screamed in one voice.

"Let's go get some," Lisa said, already heading toward the door. "My treat."

"No, you treated last time," Amy said. "It's my turn to treat."

"No, I want to treat!" Shanon said. "I never get to treat!"

"You just won an election!" Palmer argued. "I'm going to treat."

The four friends were still arguing—and laughing—as they walked arm in arm out to the ice cream truck.

CHAPTER SEVENTEEN

Dear John,

    I have a feeling you and I have hit the wall writing about music and poetry all the time, and maybe we should try some other subjects. The first, most fascinating, subject that comes to my mind is me, myself, and I! So I thought you might be interested in hearing about some of the places I've lived, like Australia and Thailand and New York City. Even though I like going to Alma Stephens, I do miss the big city sometimes. There's always something exciting going on there. You can step out of your apartment at three in the morning (not that my parents would ever let me do that!), and there will still be people walking all around on the streets! Also, in New York you're not regarded as weird if you like to make personal statements with your clothes (something you may have noticed I definitely like to do). In fact, you're considered a little weird if you don't!

Anyway, I could go on and on about myself, but first I want to ask you to write back and tell me if you think that's interesting. Also, I'd like you to tell me more about yourself. You've got to be more interesting than the weather!

Your pen pal,
Amy

Dear Amy,
I agree with you that you are an interesting subject to write letters about. Tell me more! It sounds like you've had a very unusual and exciting life. Mine's been much more ordinary, but I'll tell you about it anyway. I've lived in one place—Boston, Mass.—my whole life, but I really like it. I also like to wear clothes that other people sometimes think are a little strange. In fact, I make it a point never to wear socks that match. Today I have on one brown sock and one blue one. Not everything in life has to conform, does it?
Let me know your opinions about this.

Your pen pal,
John

P.S. You, too, are far more interesting than the weather!

Dear Sam,
Thank you so much for the great time I had at the carnival. The boat ride was fun—even though I was so

scared of the alligators! Maybe we can come up with a way for you to get invited to the next event Alma Stephens has with Ardsley. Start thinking about it now.

> *Thanks again,*
> *Palmer*

Dear Palmer,

   Thanks for your thank-you note, but I think I should be the one thanking you. I had a great time, and now all my friends want to know who that terrific-looking girl was. (I'm not telling them, though—I want to keep you all to myself!) I can hardly wait to see you again and hope we can figure out a way of getting together soon. Until then, let's keep writing letters!

> *Your pen pal for a long time, I hope,*
> *Sam*

Dear Rob,

   You must think I'm a real creep for not writing and then asking you for a favor and not even bothering to mention any of your problems. Well, you're right—and I'm truly sorry. I don't know what came over me. I can only assume that I was possessed by the Student Council election campaign and temporarily became another person. But what that "other" person did was truly rude, and I'd like to take this opportunity to apologize for her.

Seriously, I definitely do want you for a pen pal. I hope you'll forgive and forget and write back soon.

Humbly yours,
Lisa

Dear Lisa,

I accept your apology! Ever since I wrote you that last angry letter, I've been sweating it out over here, wondering what you'd write back—or if you'd write back! You'd gotten so busy that I thought you might not really care about writing to me anymore, and I got a little bent out of shape. But anyway, now we can put it behind us—maybe we'll even laugh about it someday.

I've also made up with Mars. I realize I've been a little envious of him for having so many friends in here all the time and still acing all his subjects. He's promised to try to keep the noise level down to a minimum. So now I've got my pen pal and my best buddy back again!

I know you'll write back soon!

Love,
Rob

Dear Mars,

This letter is really a thank-you note. I just know I couldn't have won the election without all your help—your nice, funny letters, the campaign buttons, and just everything you did to talk me out of being scared. I feel like I've really learned a lot lately about myself and my friends (Lisa and I have finally made up, and I'm so relieved!), but I've also learned a lot about you. Mostly I've learned that you're terrific!

Thanks again,
Shanon

Dear Shanon,

I think you're terrific for writing and telling me I'm terrific. But I thought you were terrific before that, too. The reason it was so easy for me to help you with the election was that I always knew you could do it! But I know you weren't always so sure, and I'm proud of you for seeing it through.

I'm glad you made up with Lisa, too. She's the one who thought up this pen pal plan, wasn't she? If it wasn't for her, you and I would never have met. None of the Foxes would have met any of the Unknowns. Now who could stay mad at a girl who has great ideas like that?

Your proud pen pal,
Mars

PEN PALS

Something to write home about . . .
a new Pen Pals story!

In Book Eight, the Ardsley and Alma drama departments join forces to produce a rock musical and Lisa and Amy audition for it. They both get parts, but it's Amy who gets the leading role. Lisa can't help feeling jealous, especially since her pen pal Rob lands a leading role, too—opposite Amy!

Here is a scene from Pen Pals #8: SEALED WITH A KISS

Shanon broke off in mid-sentence at the sound of a quick knock at the door. Brenda Smith came bounding in. "Somebody just told me that the cast list is up for *Everypeople*," she cried. "It's on the bulletin board at Booth Hall!"

"Oh, my gosh!" said Lisa. "Who's on the list? Do you know yet?"

"I haven't seen it yet," replied Brenda. "All I know is that Gina Hawkins was on her way to post the announcement five minutes ago."

Amy's heart began to thump. "Let's go," she said.

"I hope you all get parts," Shanon said excitedly.

"Me, too," added Palmer. "I hope that every person who wants to be in *Everypeople* gets in. But now, if you'll excuse me, I'm going to think about my dream date."

Lisa and Amy were already dashing out of the suite, with Brenda close at their heels. They made it over to Booth Hall in record time, but a large crowd had already formed in front of the bulletin board.

"Who's Everyman?" cried Muffin Talbot. The shortest girl in the class, she was jumping up and down trying to see the list.

"Some third-form boy I've never heard of," Dolores Countee replied. Lisa stood on tiptoe to peer over the tall redhead's shoulder.

"Excuse me," Amy said squeezing in. "Can we please see?"

"Oh, my gosh!" screamed Dawn Hubbard. "There's my name!"

"What part did you get?" Muffin asked.

"Home!" said Dawn. "I hope that's one of the characters with a solo!"

Lisa was breathing hard by the time she pushed her

way to the front. Amy was standing right beside her. There were two cast lists, one for Alma and the other for Ardsley.

"I can't believe it!" Lisa gasped. Rob's name was staring her right in the face. It was on top of the boys' list. "He got the lead!" she cried. "Rob's playing Everyman! I knew it would happen! I knew it!"

"You're not going to believe this either," Amy whispered in a shocked voice. Her eyes were glued to the girls' list. She nudged Lisa. "Look! We've both got parts!"

"Yippee!" yelled Lisa, moving over. "That's incredible! Rob and I—"

Her voice broke off sharply when she caught sight of her own name. It was written under the chorus! Her disbelieving eyes flew back to the top of the list.

"There must be some mistake!" She gasped.

Amy turned to her wide-eyed. "I'm in a state of shock, too," she said.

"*You* got it, Amy!" Lisa cried. "*You* got the part of Everywoman! But you weren't even trying out for it!"

Amy smiled sheepishly. "Weird, huh? I guess Gina must have thought I was right for it. Yippee! Isn't this amazing!"

"Yeah." Lisa gulped. "Congratulations." She wanted to be happy for Amy but it wasn't easy.

"Congratulations, Amy!" Brenda said, coming up behind them. "I got a part, too! I'm playing Soul! It's the part I wanted!"

"It's the part *I* wanted, too," said Amy.

"But you got an even better part," Brenda exclaimed. "You got Everywoman!" Then she turned her blue eyes on Lisa. "Congratulations, Lisa. You're playing Beauty, right?"

Lisa forced a smile.

"You'll probably get a fabulous costume," gushed Brenda. "With a name like Beauty, they'll have to make you look beautiful."

"Congratulations, everybody!" said Dawn, joining the group. "I'm playing the part of Home. From what I hear, Home is the nicest character in Gina's whole play and instead of singing rock, she sings a folk song."

"Interesting," said Muffin. "I can't wait to read the full script! I'm going to be Accomplishments—whatever that means!"

Lisa felt herself zoning out while the conversation buzzed all around her. Everybody seemed so happy. Even the people who hadn't gotten parts were being good sports about it. But she didn't feel like being a good sport. She was disappointed and even a little embarrassed. She had tried so hard to get the part of Everywoman. She even borrowed that Middle Ages costume! And now Amy, who hadn't even *wanted* the part, had gotten it!

"Too bad John didn't make it," Amy said as the crowd began to drift away.

"What?" said Lisa distractedly.

"John didn't get a part," said Amy. "You're lucky Rob did. You'll get to see him all the time at rehearsals."

"I guess," Lisa said, trying to look on the bright side.

Amy touched her arm. "Hey, I'm sorry. I know how much you wanted to be Everywoman."

"Who cares?" bluffed Lisa. "We don't even know what the play is about. We probably never will. It sounds awfully intellectual."

Amy pointed toward the snack bar. "Choc-shot?" she offered. "My treat."

"No, thanks," Lisa said, ducking away. "I . . . I've got stuff to do!"

Batting back tears, she dashed out of the building. *At least I got a part!* she thought. *And Rob did too! Things could always be worse.* But telling herself that didn't make Lisa feel any better. First Shanon had beaten her out for dorm rep, and now Amy had beaten her out of the part of Everywoman! Worst of all, Amy would be playing opposite Rob! In the play, Everyman and Everywoman were boyfriend and girlfriend. Now, instead of being *her* boyfriend, Rob would be spending all his time pretending to be Amy's!

Lisa doesn't like feeling this way, but she can't seem to help it. No matter how hard she tries, each day she feels worse. Will Lisa's jealousy destroy her friendships with her pen pal Rob and Amy? And will Amy and Rob learn of Lisa's feelings before it's too late?

P.S. Have you missed any Pen Pals? Catch up now!

PEN PALS #1: BOYS WANTED!

Suitemates Lisa, Shanon, Amy, and Palmer love the Alma Stephens School for Girls. There's only one problem—no boys! So the girls put an ad in the newspaper of the nearby Ardsley Academy for Boys asking for male pen pals. Soon their mailboxes are flooded with letters and photos from Ardsley boys, but the girls choose four boys from a suite just like their own. Through their letters, the girls learn a lot about their new pen pals—and about themselves.

PEN PALS #2: TOO CUTE FOR WORDS

Palmer, the rich girl from Florida, has never been one for playing by the rules. So when she wants Amy's pen pal, Simmie, instead of her own, she simply takes him. She writes to Simmie secretly and soon he stops writing to Amy. When Shanon, Lisa, and Amy find out why, the suite is in an uproar. How could Palmer be so deceitful? Before long, Palmer is thinking of leaving the suite—and the other girls aren't about to stop her. Where will it all end?

PEN PALS #3: P.S. FORGET IT!

Palmer is out to prove that her pen pal is the best—and her suitemate Lisa's is a jerk. When Lisa receives strange letters and a mysterious prank gift, it looks as if Palmer may be right. But does she have to be so smug about it? Soon it's all-out war in Suite 3-D!

From the sidelines, Shanon and Amy think something fishy is going on. Is the pen pal scheme going too far? Will it stop before Lisa does something she may regret? Or will the girls learn to settle their differences?

PEN PALS #4: NO CREEPS NEED APPLY

Palmer takes up tennis so she can play in the Alma–Ardsley tennis tournament with her pen pal, Simmie Randolph III. Lisa helps coach Palmer, and soon Palmer has come so far that they are both proud of her. But when Palmer finds herself playing *against*—not *with*—her super-competitive pen pal, she realizes that winning the game could mean losing *him*!

Palmer wants to play her best, and her suitemates will think she's a real creep if she lets down the school. Is any boy worth the loss of her friends?

PEN PALS #5: SAM THE SHAM

Palmer has a new pen pal. His name is Sam O'Leary, and he seems absolutely perfect! Palmer is walking on air. She can't think or talk about anything but Sam—even when she's supposed to be tutoring Gabby, a third-grader from town, as part of the school's community-service requirement. Palmer thinks it's a drag, until she realizes just how much she means to little Gabby. And just in time, too—she needs something to distract her from her own problems when it appears that there *is* no Sam O'Leary at Ardsley. But if that's the truth—who *has* been writing to Palmer?

PEN PALS #6: AMY'S SONG

The Alma Stephens School is buzzing with excitement—the girls are going to London! Amy is most excited of all. She and her pen pal John have written a song together, and one of the Ardsley boys has arranged for her to sing it in a London club. It's the chance of a lifetime! But once in London, the girls are constantly supervised, and Amy can't see how she'll ever get away to the club. She and her suite-mates plot and scheme to get out from under the watchful eye of their chaperone, but it's harder than they thought it would be. It looks as if Amy will never get her big break!

WANTED: BOYS — AND GIRLS —
WHO CAN WRITE !

Join the Pen Pals Exchange and get a pen pal of your own!
Fill out the form below.

Send it with a self-addressed stamped envelope to:

PEN PALS EXCHANGE
c/o The Trumpet Club
PO Box 632
Holmes, PA 19043
U.S.A.

In a couple of weeks you'll receive the name and address
of someone who wants to be your pen pal.

Cut here --

PEN PALS EXCHANGE

NAME _____ GRADE _____

ADDRESS _____

TOWN _____ STATE _____ ZIP _____

DON'T FORGET TO INCLUDE A STAMPED ENVELOPE
WITH YOUR NAME AND ADDRESS ON IT!